FALLING FOR MURDER

A Bobwhite Mountain Cozy Mystery

Book 2

Jamie Rutland Gillespie

2022 Falling for Murder
Jamie Rutland Gillespie

Library of Congress Control Number: 2022910485

For my precious daughter, Meghan. You are the greatest blessing I have ever received. I am forever grateful that God let me be your Mom. I'm so very proud of you and I love you with all my heart.

Love,
Mom

Inheriting Murder Book 1
Falling for Murder Book 2

Chapter 1

It was a gorgeous day in Bobwhite Mountain, Tennessee. There was a crispness in the air which signified the beginning of fall in the mountain town. The early September weather was perfect and the leaves on the trees were beginning their transformation into wonderful shades of orange, red and yellow.

Landry Burke was pleased to now be a resident of this quaint town. Her Aunt Tildie had passed away earlier this year and Landry had been the sole beneficiary to her aunt's estate, which meant she now owned the apartment building on Main Street called Magnolia Place, as well as the bookstore across the street, Jasmine Bloom Books. The bookstore was where she was headed this morning.

Ms. Millie had been Aunt Tildie's best friend for many years and was the manager of the bookstore. She was away for two weeks visiting her daughter, Vanessa Woodward, and her family in Mississippi. Vanessa was married to a very successful attorney and they had three children. Ms. Millie was thrilled to have grandchildren and tried to visit a couple of times a year.

Landry was filling in for Ms. Millie at the bookstore and would work every day until 3:30 when the part time clerk arrived from school. Maisy was a sophomore this year and was a hard worker. She and Landry had bonded awhile back over a situation and Landry thought a lot of Maisy. Jenna, the other employee of the bookstore, had graduated high school and was working full time now. This not only helped Jenna out with college funds but also took a load off of Ms. Millie.

When Landry walked into the bookstore, Jenna was already there getting the register ready for the day.

"Hi, Miss Landry. I already started the coffeepot. I knew that was the first thing you would want me to do." Jenna smiled.

"You know it, Jenna." Landry winked at her and headed to the back office to put her purse up.

About that time, the phone rang in the bookstore. Landry reached for it and told Jenna that she had it.

Without any preamble, Ms. Millie said, "I just wanted to be sure that you were there and opened up. I always open up right on time, ya know."

"Ms. Millie, I do own this store, you know. I am not going to be late opening up." Landry rolled her eyes.

"Don't backtalk me. I don't have the energy to argue with you today. I have had a terrible thing happen to me." Ms. Millie sounded put upon.

"You have only been there a week. You still have another week to go. What's happened in one week that has made you all upset?" Landry asked as she poured her coffee, holding the phone with her shoulder.

"My bracelet. My beautiful diamond bracelet that Clive gave me for our anniversary the year before he passed away. It's gone." Ms. Millie informed Landry.

"Gone? Did you lose it?" Landry asked. "I sure hope you didn't lose it on the bus you insisted you take to

Mississippi. I tried so hard to let me take you halfway and for Vanessa to meet us and pick you up. Those buses are packed with people and I didn't want you on one of them. I worried myself sick until you called and told me you got there safely," Landry reminded her.

"Stop rambling, child. I didn't lose it on the bus. I wore it for a couple of days before it went missing. Besides, if you and Vanessa had just let me drive my own self here you wouldn't have had to worry about all those people on the bus." Ms. Millie sounded aggravated now.

Landry let out a loud sigh and said, "No. I would have had to worry about your car breaking down and you being stuck in the middle of nowhere at night. Anyway, where do you think you lost the bracelet?"

"I am trying to tell you if you would just listen. I did not lose it. It was stolen," Ms. Millie announced.

"Stolen? What are you talking about? Did you or Vanessa file a police report? When did it happen?" Landry asked.

"No. I did not file a report. I'm about to have my own grandchild put in jail. His father is a prominent attorney in this town. How would that look?" Ms. Millie was whispering so Landry assumed someone else was near the phone.

"Your grandson?! Why would he steal your bracelet? Surely he knew he wouldn't get away with it?"

"It was Wesley, the oldest one. He's a teenager now, you know. Just turned 13 last week. He had some of his friends over for a party in the backyard. I know it couldn't have been one of the other boys since it was missing before the party. I am just sick to my stomach, Landry. How can my own grandchild be a thief at just 13 years old? He is on the evil path." Ms. Millie sounded like she was crying.

"Maybe it's just a misunderstanding. Maybe Vanessa took the bracelet to have more diamonds added or something. Try to calm down, Ms. Millie. I'm sure it will turn up." Landry couldn't believe that Wesley would steal from Ms. Millie. She had met him when he and his Dad were passing through Bobwhite Mountain to a travel ballgame. They stopped and had lunch with her and Ms. Millie. He seemed like a nice, polite child. His manners were impeccable.

At that moment, Ms. Millie raised her voice really high and said, "Landry, I am on vacation spending valuable time with my family. I don't have time to walk you through the computer program. You have to learn these things for yourself. Now, I have to go."

Click. Dial tone. Landry assumed that Vanessa had walked in.

Jenna walked into the back office and told Landry that someone needed help finding a book and that she was already busy with another customer. Landry put her coffee down and walked up front to help.

She saw a customer with her back to her. She was wearing a scarf on her head and was short and tiny. Landry looked around and noticed that there was not another person in the bookstore except Jenna. Landry wondered if the other customer had left already. She cleared her throat and said, "Could I help you with something?"

The woman with the scarf answered in a low, gravelly voice. "Yes, you can. You can come over there and give me a big ole hug!"

Landry looked at Jenna and she just shrugged her shoulders and looked out the window like the woman hadn't said anything strange. About that time, the woman pulled the scarf off of her head and turned around to look at Landry.

"Oh, my goodness. Annie, what are you doing here?" Landry asked. In front of her stood her best friend in the whole world. Annie's hair was still cut in the pixie cut that looked so good on her, although now it was a bright blue instead of the hot pink that it was the last time Landry saw her that day she had packed up and left Bent Branch, SC for the hills of Tennessee to claim her inheritance.

"Surprise!" Annie screamed. She bounced over to Landry and grabbed her in a tight embrace. "I was going to call you before I came but it seemed like every time I picked up the phone, something would happen at the bakery that would make me wonder if I really would get the time away to visit. Finally, I decided that I would just jump in the car and drive here."

"I'm so happy to see you. How long can you stay?" Landry was grinning from ear to ear as she squeezed Annie tight.

"A week. You remember Mrs. Winfield, don't you? She has always stalked me to sell the bakery to her. She works for me part-time but keeps asking me to sell the place to her. I've told her no over and over. Anyway, she's going to work full time this week so that I can have some time off. We don't have any special occasions to bake for and she's a great worker," Annie explained.

Landry looked at Jenna. "You Stinker! You fooled me," she laughed.

"I had to Miss Landry. Annie told me that she wanted to surprise you and I wanted to help her do just that." Jenna giggled.

"Well, I'm glad you did. This is the best surprise ever. Do you think you can handle things here so that I can take Annie to my apartment and get her settled?" Landry asked her.

"Of course I can. Don't worry about working here today. Maisy will be in at 3:30, and I can take care of anything before then," Jenna assured her.

Landry looked towards the front door and frowned. "Uh-oh. There's Cecil. He's early today and I haven't brought the mail from the office for him to pick up."

Jenna came out behind the counter and said, "I'll run back to the office and get it. Is it in the basket already?"

"Yes. I put it in there yesterday afternoon. Thank you, Jenna," Landry said just as Cecil walked in with his perennial frown on his face. Landry couldn't figure out why he was always in a bad mood.

"Hi, Cecil. Gorgeous day out today. Jenna's gone to the office to get our mail for you. How's your day been so far?" Landry decided to kill him with kindness and see if that worked on his mood a little.

"What's so gorgeous about it? No matter the weather, I still have to pick up and carry all those heavy boxes you send out of here. I've told you that those need to be lighter for me to be able to carry them without straining my back." Cecil stared at her with that mean look on his face.

Jenna walked back up to the front with the little bit of mail they had for him today. "Here you are, Cecil. Very light load today."

"About time. Who is this person with blue hair? My wife had blue hair one time when her hairdresser was trying to color her grays up for her. I told my wife when she came back home with that awful colored hair that we should sue. I guess you should, too, young lady." He stood there waiting for an answer.

Landry cleared her throat and said, "Cecil, this is my best friend, Annie. She's from South Carolina and has come to visit for the week. She likes her hair this color. She did it intentionally."

Annie smiled at Cecil with a tight smile and said, "Pleased to meet ya."

"Um hmm. I have to go now." He turned around and left with no further comment.

After a second, Landry, Jenna and Annie burst out laughing. "What is his problem?" Annie asked. "I feel bad for him. He seems like a miserable old man."

Jenna looked thoughtful and then spoke up. "You know, Ms. Millie told me that years ago, Cecil and his wife, Dinky, had twin daughters that they both doted on. She said those twins were like little porcelain dolls when they were toddlers. Then, when they were teenagers, they were not only gorgeous but they both were accomplished athletes at the high school. One night, they were coming back from a soccer game and their car went down an embankment. They were both killed. Ms. Millie said that Cecil has never been the same. She said that Dinky was devastated, of course, but that she learned to go on with life. Cecil just got sad, angry and grumpy."

"I didn't know that," Landry said. "I do know that everyone handles grief differently. I'll try to be kinder to Cecil now. That's one of the saddest things I've ever heard. He's still a grieving father after all these years. He must have loved his girls so much." She looked at the ground and thought how awful it must have been for him and Dinky to go through that.

Chapter 2

Landry and Annie walked across the street to Magnolia Place. Landry told Annie that she could come back down and move her car into the parking garage in her extra parking space. Before they could open the door to the apartment building, Garrett, one of the lobby assistants, had it open for them. They walked in and stopped so that Landry could introduce Annie.

"Hey, Annie." Lisa, who was the manager of Magnolia Place and a friend of Landry's said, "It's so nice to meet you."

Annie thanked her and then turned to Garrett who was openly staring at her blue hair. "I know. You don't like it. I change it up all the time. I love color and I change my hair depending on my mood."

"On the contrary, Miss…uh, I'm sorry I didn't get your last name," Garrett said.

Annie said, "Please just call me Annie."

Landry laughed and said, "Good try, Annie, but that's a no go. Garrett is of the old school and insists on calling women by their last names. Well, except for Lisa. I have no idea how she got him to call her by her first name but I'm on a quest to find out."

Lisa made the motion of zipping her lips and throwing away the key. "I'll never reveal that." She smiled at Garrett.

"Okay, then." Annie looked confused but said,

"Dearson. My last name is Dearson, Garrett."

Garrett turned his head to the side a little and nodded. "On the contrary, Miss Dearson. Blue is my favorite color and your hair looks fine to me. Nothing wrong with being unique."

Lisa and Landry stood there with their mouths hanging open.

"Since when?" They both said at the same time.

Garrett just looked at them and gave a small smile. "Do you have any luggage to bring in, Miss Dearson?"

"Nope. I'll get it later," Annie said as she waved at Garrett and Lisa bounced on her heels over to the elevator. She really did look like a little pixie fairy. "See y'all later."

"Lisa, I've been meaning to ask you. Have we rented Diane Huffman's apartment since she moved out to her new house?" Landry looked at Lisa.

"Yes, we did, and now we have another empty apartment," Lisa said.

"What? Who moved out now?" Landry asked.

Lisa laughed, "Well, nobody. Glenn Mayhew just got married and his wife, Erin, works from home and has told him that she'll move here to Bobwhite Mountain only if he gets a two bedroom apartment. He loves it here since it's right in the middle of the district he works in for the security company. So, he wants the two bedroom apartment that Diane vacated on the second floor. His one bedroom on your floor will now be available."

"I see. That's wonderful, since Glenn is such a great resident here. I'm so happy for his marriage and that he and his wife will be living here. Thanks for arranging all of that, Lisa," Landry told her and said goodbye.

Landry walked over to wait with Annie and as the elevator doors opened, she saw Mr. Larson, who lived on the 2nd floor, in his wheelchair with Mary Goode pushing him. Mr. Larson had been in a car accident recently and Mary, who lived in an apartment on the 3rd floor and was a private caregiver, was taking care of him until he recovered.

Landry smiled at them both and introduced Annie to them. "I guess you two are going to take advantage of this wonderful day we are having."

"We sure are. We're going to the park to sit and people watch and then we're going to stop by K&L and grab a bite to eat," Mary said, referring to the K&L diner on Main Street. "I don't have any other clients today, so we are just going to enjoy the gorgeous weather."

Mr. Larson looked up at her, smiled and said, "It sure is good to have somebody to go eat with. I always just get takeout since I'm alone most of the time. I'm really looking forward to today."

They all told each other goodbye and Landry and Annie headed to Landry's apartment on the 4th floor.

"You're right, Lan. Everybody here seems so nice and caring. I see why you love it here." Annie smiled.

When they walked into the apartment, Landry's YorkiePom, Zep, came running into the living room from the den. Zep thought the den was his own private room and spent most of his time there if he wasn't on Landry's bed.

He immediately stopped in his tracks when he saw Annie. He walked up to her and sniffed her leg. Then, the barking started. He barked and yipped and spun around and around. Annie reached down to pet him and he backed away and growled at her.

"What in the world?" Landry said. "He fawns over everybody. He won't leave them alone if they don't have him in their lap. Why's he so upset with you?"

"I don't know. I love animals. You know that," Annie said as she sat down on the floor and called Zep to come let her pet him. He started towards her and then he jumped back and growled again. This time was more menacing than the first.

Annie looked like she would cry. "He's so adorable. I don't know why he hates me."

"He doesn't hate you. I just can't figure it out. He's such a loving doggie. The only thing that he's ever growled at was a cat. He detests cats. In fact, I worry all the time that I'm going to be taking him out for a walk one day and Mrs. Harrington, who lives on the 3rd floor, will be in the lobby with her cat. She has a Maine coon cat named Peaches that's bigger than Zep. I've seen it a couple of times but Zep wasn't with me."

"That's it." Annie jumped up and Zep growled at her again. "I stopped right outside of town to get me something to drink. I was so thirsty. Anyway, I ran into this little coffee shop and the owner had a cat in there. She said the cat was named 'Aroma' and was the mascot of the place. She was so adorable and I petted her and she just purred. I did wash my hands before I got the drink but as I was leaving the place, Aroma came up and rubbed against my legs. She was so loving. I'm going to hit the showers and hopefully Zep will calm down. Do you have something I can put on?" She looked at Landry.

"I'll grab you some sweats for now. When you move your car into the garage, we'll bring your things up," Landry told her.

Annie got her shower and put on the fresh clothes. She walked slowly into the den where Landry and Zep were watching TV. She sat down in a chair and said, "Come on, Zep. Come to Aunt Annie."

Zep just stared at her at first but then walked over and sniffed her. As soon as he found out she didn't smell like a cat, he jumped in her lap and licked her face.

Annie looked thrilled. She hugged him and petted him and called him cuddly names. They were enamored with each other.

"Well, that mystery is solved," said Landry. "If only I could find Ms. Millie's bracelet that easily before she accuses her grandson of larceny."

"Huh?" Annie looked confused.

Landry said, "I'll explain all that over lunch. Let's go to the Takeout King. They have a dine-in area despite their name. I will ask Adam if he wants to join us. He loves the food there," she said, referring to Adam Wilcox, her aunt's attorney and Landry's good friend.

"I have to move my car first and bring up my luggage. I'm not going out in public with sweatpants on. This is my first time in town and I at least want people to think I know how to dress." Annie turned on her heels and grabbed her keys. "I'll be right back as soon as I move the car."

Landry called Adam and asked if he wanted to meet her and Annie for lunch. He did and they settled on a time. She walked over and turned on some music and opened the balcony drapes. She was admiring the mountain in the distance when Annie came back. She was not alone.

"Wyatt. What are you doing here?" Landry smiled and went over to give him a hug hello. He was the sheriff of Bobwhite Mountains and another one of Landry's close friends.

"I was downstairs in the lobby getting Lisa to call up to you to see if I could drop by for a second and this blue-haired young lady said she needed me to help her with her luggage." He laughed.

"I told him who I was and that I was staying with you for the week," Annie said righteously. "I didn't just ask a strange man to help me. I overheard Lisa calling him Wyatt and I remembered that he was the sheriff in these parts."

Annie took the luggage from him and proceeded to move it all to one of the two spare bedrooms in the apartment. Landry had told her to pick the one she wanted since both of them had been furnished after Landry moved in and the hall bath served both rooms.

"What's up, Wyatt?" Landry asked him.

He looked anxious and worried as he told her, "We seem to have a missing person. Carla Hanson works at the bank as a teller. She didn't show up for work today and we've checked with her friends and family. Nobody has seen her since she left the bank Friday afternoon. She had mentioned to a few people that she was going out of town for the weekend, but nobody has heard from her since she left work. Her parents live over in Wrigley Springs but Carla lives here in Bobwhite Mountain and works at the bank. She rents a small studio apartment from an elderly couple. Her apartment is in the back part of their property. They say they haven't seen or heard anything suspicious since Friday."

Annie walked back in the room and sat down. Wyatt looked at her and said, "Annie, I like to bounce things off of Landry and best friend Adam, to get their opinions of some of my cases since they were helpful in the last big case I handled. I hope I can depend on your discretion and that you understand that nothing I say is to be repeated to anyone." He waited for Annie to nod her head and then he continued.

"Thing is, though, we haven't found her car. It seems to have disappeared, too. None of her credit cards have been used since before she went missing."

"Does she have any history of leaving without letting someone know? I mean, I know she's an adult, but some people do have the habit of dropping out of sight sometimes," Landry asked him.

"Not according to everyone I've questioned so far. In fact, they say that she is the most punctual and dependable person they know." Wyatt sighed and stood up.

"I have to get going. I just wanted to see if you might

happen to know her or anything about her. Since Lisa's roommate, Hannah, is a teller at the bank, I asked Lisa about Carla. She said that she's only seen Carla when she was in the bank doing business and hasn't even heard Hannah speak of her. I had already questioned Hannah along with all of the other bank employees and she said much the same. She told me that she and Carla didn't associate outside of work but that they never had any problems, either. I also talked to Diane Huffman who is the Assistant Bank Manager and she had no information that might help us.

Landry looked concerned and said, "Diane actually lived here in the building for a while. She purchased a home and moved out recently. She seems like a hard worker from what I've seen. I sure hope Carla turns up soon, Wyatt. That worries me that nobody has seen or heard from her since Friday."

"The other teller besides Hannah and Carla is Jill Boatwright, Lenny's wife," Wyatt said.

Lenny was one of Landry's maintenance guys for Magnolia Place. She had met Jill and really liked her.

"What did Jill have to say about Carla?" she asked Wyatt.

Wyatt shook his head. "Nothing yet. I saw Lenny and told him that I needed to talk to Jill about all of this just to see what insight she might have. Lenny said Jill left right after work on Friday, too. She went with their son, Les, to a Boy Scout retreat. Lenny said he probably could find them but that no cell phones worked up in the back mountains where they were camping. I told him to just get Jill to come see me when they get back. It's a weeklong camping trip. He said they're due back on Friday next week."

Wyatt turned to her. "We'll be holding a press conference this afternoon. Her parents are going to be speaking and asking anyone with any information to come forward. Since she's been missing for over 48 hours, we'll get some help searching for her from the missing persons groups around the country. Her parents and friends have also made fliers and will be putting those up today after the presser."

They said their goodbyes and promised to get together soon. Landry and Annie went down to the garage to get Landry's car and go to the Takeout King to meet Adam.

When they walked into the restaurant, Adam was already at a table and waved them over.

Landry walked towards him with Annie following. When they got to the table, Landry said, "Hi, Adam. This is my best friend in the entire world, Annie." Landry pulled Annie close to her.

"Hey, Annie. It's so good to meet you. I know Landry's excited you're visiting. She talks about you and the adventures you two had in Bent Branch all the time." Adam smiled and that adorable dimple popped out in his cheek.

"Hi, Adam. Nice to meet ya and, yes, I'm thrilled to be here with Landry. We have a lot to catch up on," Annie said as they all sat down and picked up the menus.

Kylie Tillson, the owner's daughter, came over to take

their orders. "Hey, Landry, Adam and–"

"Oh, Kylie, this is my friend, Annie. Annie, Kylie, is the owner, Terrance Tillson's daughter. Everyone calls him TT." Landry turned to Kylie and asked her, "How's college going?"

"Just fine. I actually love it way more than high school. Now, what can I get y'all to eat?" She took out her pencil and notebook.

They gave her their orders and as she walked away, Landry's phone rang. She looked at the caller ID and sighed. "Ms. Millie," she said to Adam and walked outside to take the call.

"Hey, Ms. Millie. I hope things are going well in Mississippi," Landry said, knowing that would not be the case.

"Huh. No, they are not. I'm still missing my bracelet. I just cannot believe that my own grandson is a thief. He has always been such a model child. Good grades, perfect manners, never talks back. I'm just so upset about this, Landry." Ms. Millie moaned.

"Ms. Millie, you don't know that Wesley took your bracelet. You could've lost it or just misplaced it. Please don't accuse him until you've looked into it further," Landry pleaded.

She heard Ms. Millie saying something to someone else. "No no, Paige. That's sticky. Don't do that. Why in the world would your Mama give you a sucker to eat in the house where you can get it on the furniture? Stop that…no! Don't do that."

"What is she doing, Ms. Millie?"

"Oh no. My clueless daughter gave Paige, you know the littlest one of the kids, a sucker and Paige has slobbered it on everything. Now, she has gotten it stuck to my knee high hose." Ms. Millie sounded disgusted.

"It has to still be hot in Mississippi right now, Ms. Millie. Why on earth would you be wearing hose?" Landry asked.

"They are just my knee high ones, Landry. I never wear a frock without some sort of hose. That is so unlady-like. Right now, I have to go. This sucker is stuck to my hose and Paige is sticky all over. What a mess." Landry heard Ms. Millie yelling for Vanessa.

"Vanessa, come get this child and put her in the bath. What in tarnation were you thinking of giving her a sucker in the house and letting her crawl everywhere? I have to try to pull this sticky thing off of my hose. I know it's gonna cause a hole in them," Ms. Millie said.

"I have to go, Landry. This place is like a three ring circus. I know I didn't raise my daughter to run a house this way," Ms. Millie said and hung up the phone.

Landry shook her head and walked back into the Takeout King. Adam looked at her and said, "So, how is Ms. Millie's vacation going with Vanessa and her family?"

Landry gave him a "you don't even want to know" look and said, "Let's just say that Vanessa probably won't be too sad to see the hind end of Ms. Millie heading back to Bobwhite Mountain."

They all laughed, said the blessing and started eating.

Annie was raving about how good the food was when Wyatt walked in the door. Annie waved him over to their table.

"Hey Wyatt. I thought you would be too busy to eat lunch out. Have a seat and join us."

"I'm just picking up my takeout order to eat in the office," Wyatt said, as he sat down. "I saw yours and Adam's cars outside and decided to come inside to pick it up."

He turned to Annie and said, "How are you liking our little town so far?"

"I'm loving it. I now know why Landry raved about it so much. It has that small town feel just like Bent Branch. I've visited large cities before and I felt so claustrophobic with all of the people packed into everywhere I went. Bobwhite Mountain is such a nice place." Annie said, as Kylie brought Wyatt's takeout order over.

He got up and whispered to the others, "I have to go. We are having that press conference in about two hours. Everybody in town will be on edge after that. I sure hope we find her soon."

As he walked out the door, Adam said, "I take it he has already told you both about Carla."

"Yes. I'm so worried about it," Landry said with a frown.

They finished their lunch and made plans to meet at Landry's apartment one night for a home cooked meal. Adam left to go to an appointment and Landry and Annie headed back home.

Chapter 3

The next few days went by, with Landry showing Annie around town and introducing her to the people they met. Everyone was on edge because of Carla's disappearance. She still hadn't been found and her car was still missing.

On Thursday, they were both at the bookstore with Jenna when the mail came in. A new person brought the mail in and asked if they had any to go out. Jenna told him yes and went to the back office to get it.

"Hi. I don't think we've met." Landry offered her a greeting. "I'm Landry Burke and this is my bookstore. I also own Magnolia Place, the apartment building across the street," Landry said. "Where is Cecil today?"

"Hi. Nice to meet you," he said as he shook her hand. "I'm Carter Morris. I've worked for the post office for several years but usually I work another route. Cecil fell yesterday and broke his leg and his collarbone. Poor guy, he'll be laid up for a long time. I wouldn't be surprised if he retires after this." Jenna handed him the outgoing mail, which included several large boxes.

Carter grabbed two of the boxes and went outside to put them in the mail truck. He came back in and got the other two along with the regular mail. He was a lot younger and stronger than Cecil, Landry noted.

"Oh no, I'm so sorry about Cecil. I know this has to be hard work for him to do now that he's getting on up in years. I'll be sure to put him on our prayer list at church. I might go over to visit him and Dinky and take them a cake or something." Landry shook her head.

"Well, actually when Dinky called to tell us about Cecil's accident, she asked that we not come to visit right now. She said that Cecil is having a hard time accepting that he's practically bedridden for the time being. You know how grumpy Cecil is on a regular basis, so I'm sure Dinky doesn't want people coming in and out and aggravating him even more. Bless her heart, she'll probably need a vacation after Cecil is fully healed," he laughed.

"I didn't even think about that. Of course she doesn't want to deal with lots of folks coming in and out. I'll just send Cecil a get well card. Thanks for letting me know, Carter." Landry held the door open for him as he went back to the mail truck.

"Wow, that's sad," Jenna said. "I know Cecil is grumpy, but I'm so used to seeing him every day. Deep down, I think he's a nice man. He reminds me of my grandpa who is grouchy all the time but would do anything in the world for me."

Annie and Landry nodded and walked to the back office. Annie spoke up, "That's awful that he injured himself so bad. He's fortunate to have a wife to take care of him, though."

Landry poured them each a cup of coffee and said, "He sure is. Dinky was a nurse in her younger years, so he's in good hands. I know it'll be tiring for her, though."

Landry's phone rang. She looked at it and hit "answer". "Hi, Ms. Millie. How's it going today?"

"Don't be so perky. I'm ready to come home. These kids are just too much for me at my age. It's been raining here for three days and they can't go in the yard. School's been out all three days because of some kind stomach bug that took out half the teachers and students. Vanessa's tried to keep them busy with games, food and doing online school work with them. That takes up about two hours of the day and the rest of the time, they're underfoot screaming, crying, complaining and just plain aggravating me. I'm coming home on Saturday instead of Sunday. Can you pick me up at the bus station in Wrigley Springs at 6pm on Saturday?"

Landry was just nodding her head throughout Ms. Millie's diatribe. She was talking so fast that Landry didn't even realize when she was done.

"Child, did you hear me? Can you pick me up or not?" Ms. Millie asked impatiently.

"Oh, yes…of course I can. It'll be close to dark by that time now that the time has changed here. I'll try to be waiting so that I can help you get your things off the bus. My friend, Annie, has been visiting this week and is leaving on Saturday morning. I was hoping the two of you could meet one another but I guess it'll have to be another time," Landry told Ms. Millie.

"Yes, yes. Now, Landry, don't forget me at the bus station. I don't want to have to worry about finding somebody else to pick me up once I get there. And, sometimes there are some sketchy types hanging out there. I don't want to get mugged. I just can't wait to be alone in my house with peace and quiet." Ms. Millie was sounding anxious.

"I'll be there, Ms. Millie. I promise," Landry assured her.

Click. Ms. Millie hung up.

"Wow…Ms. Millie sounds like a character." Annie laughed.

"You have no idea." Landry drank her coffee.

When Maisy came in at 3:30 to help Jenna the rest of the day, Landry and Annie walked to Greene's Groceries to pick up some things for dinner. Adam and Wyatt were coming over to eat tonight, but since they were all planning to go to the Sky High tomorrow night to celebrate Annie's last night in Bobwhite Mountain, Landry was going to make something simple for tonight's meal. She decided on thick sliced pork chops and roasted brussel sprouts, since both of those could go in the oven at the same time. She got a bag of red potatoes and would make some potato salad to go with the meal.

Since Annie was the baker, she decided to make some pumpkin cookies to go with coffee for dessert. "Those are so easy to make and are delicious. It only takes three ingredients," she told Landry as they went to the baking aisle.

When they turned the corner, Landry spotted Drew Anderson who was the manager of the store. He and his wife, Tori, lived on the second floor of Magnolia Place. Tori was an online teacher and was such a sweet woman.

"Hi, Drew. How are things going?" Landry greeted

him.

"Hi, Landry. Things are going just great. The store is staying busy, which is how I like it. Tori just got another contract with a new company to do tutoring online in addition to her other classes that she teaches. Couldn't be better, actually. Except for the missing woman in town. Tori is afraid to walk anywhere by herself until they find out what happened to Carla. I know her from the bank. I saw her there whenever I went in to make the store's deposits. I sure hope she's found safe." Drew looked worried.

Landry nodded in agreement. "So do I. This is such a small town that I think everyone knows Carla from doing business at the bank. I hate that Tori is afraid but it's better to be cautious when things like this are going on. This is my friend, Annie. She's visiting me for the week." Landry introduced them to each other and they spoke briefly.

Drew was called to the front of the store and Landry and Annie gathered up the rest of their items. They checked out and as they were walking back to the apartment building, Landry noticed that the former art gallery was being vacated. The owner and her brother had been involved in an art heist and two murders earlier in the year.

"I wonder what business will replace the gallery," Landry said to Annie. "Truthfully, I'm glad it's gone. Every time I walked by there, I thought about that horrible night with Sylvia on my balcony."

They walked into the apartment building and Landry saw that Josh Henley was at the desk. Josh was a retired cop and he came in for his shift at noon and worked until 8pm. He was one of three full time and one part time lobby assistants for the building. Landry and Annie spoke when they walked by.

While they were waiting in the elevator, Lisa came out of the conference room behind her office. "Hey, guys. Anything interesting scheduled for today?" she asked them.

"Nope. We're going to cook dinner in my apartment for Adam and Wyatt tonight. Why don't you join us?" Landry asked Lisa.

"Sorry, I can't. I already have plans with Jarred." Lisa smiled.

Lisa had finally told them who she was dating after keeping it a secret for a long time. She and Jarred Atkins, the vet tech at Dr. Portman's Vet Clinic, were dating. They seemed to be very happy and spent a lot of time together. Adam, Wyatt and Landry had taken bets on who the mystery man was before Lisa told them. They had all lost. In fact, Landry thought it may have been Wyatt for a while.

Landry and Annie spent the rest of the day listening to music, dancing and just enjoying each other's company. Annie absolutely loved Landry's balcony. She told Landry that she needed to get some potted plants to put out there to brighten it up some. Since Landry loved flowers, she said she would do that. She just hoped she could keep them alive.

Annie looked at Landry while they were drinking their iced tea on the balcony. "Landry, since Blaine cheated on me and broke my heart, I've been thinking. Did I do something to make him stray? I mean, I thought we were in a good place. We were even talking about marriage. I've since found out that he didn't just cheat on me with one woman. There were several. How could I have been so naïve and stupid to not even have a clue?"

"Oh, Annie. What Blaine did was a reflection of his character, not yours. There's nothing you could have done differently. I spent hours and hours with the two of you while you were dating and I thought everything was perfect between you two. Anybody would be blessed to have you as a girlfriend or wife. You have to try to move on and don't lose out on a chance at true love just because you misjudged Blaine's character. We all have lots of mulligans when it comes to romance. Remember Tag that I dated in college? I thought he hung the moon. Turns out, he was a small-time drug dealer who had quit college two months before we started dating. Talk about dumb. I had no idea who he really was until we were eating out one night and the cops arrested him right in front of me at our table." Landry shook her head.

"That was crazy. I remember that you twisted your ring on your finger so much that night. You actually broke the skin that time and started bleeding from the contact rash." Annie said about one of Landry's coping mechanisms for her anxiety.

"Yep. I was so nervous and anxious. Boy, was I grateful to find out the kind of person he was before we got seriously involved, though." Landry sighed and looked at her watch.

"We better start preparing dinner and dessert. Adam and Wyatt eat like two teenage boys and they'll be hungry after a full day's work." She got up to go back inside.

Annie rose, too, and asked Landry, "I know the three of you are great friends, but do you have feelings for one or the other? I mean, like romantic feelings?"

Landry stopped in her tracks. "I don't think so. It's very complicated. They're both wonderful men, but I still think of them as my friends. The ones I can go to with anything and I know they'll help me. They were both so amazing to me when I first moved to Bobwhite Mountain. I can't imagine my life without them in it. I will admit that Adam's dimple on his cheek and his crystal clear blue eyes do make my heart flutter a little. Do not repeat that, Annie. I trust you and that's why I said that out loud to you."

Annie smiled. "Your secrets are always safe with me. I was just wondering, since they both look like little boys looking at a bag of candy when they look at you."

Landry's mouth dropped and Annie walked past her into the kitchen.

The guys arrived just as dinner was ready. They both washed up and came into the kitchen to eat. Landry plated the chops, brussel sprouts and potato salad for all of them and Annie made them all iced tea. They sat down, Adam said the blessing and they started eating.

"Wyatt, is there anything new in Carla's case? It's so hard to believe that she disappeared into thin air," Landry said.

"No. We have a BOLO out on her car but so far,

nobody's spotted it. She was a known hiker, so I even sent my deputies up to Sky High Mountain to search there, since that's a popular hiking spot. No sign of her. I didn't expect there to be, since she had told many people that she was going out of town for the weekend. I sure wish we could get a lead soon," Wyatt told them.

"Me, too. I've already talked to the husband of one of my residents in the building and she is afraid to even walk down Main Street without him being with her. I hate that people are scared in our little town," Landry said.

"Yeah, that doesn't sit well with me either." Wyatt looked angry. "People should feel safe here. I sure will be glad when we find out what's happened."

They finished their meal and Landry started a pot of coffee. They all walked out on the balcony and Zep followed. He knew that he would be getting lots of petting from "his guys". They didn't disappoint him. After being loved on, Zep went to his food bowl on the balcony and ate. He then got him some water and laid down on the floor and promptly went to sleep.

Annie went inside and got the cookies that she had made and brought everyone a cup of coffee. They sat and talked and devoured the cookies.

"These are delicious, Annie," Adam said. "I've never had pumpkin cookies with chocolate chips in them before. I love pumpkin pie and I love chocolate, though, so it makes sense that the cookies are so good."

"Thanks. I make them at the bakery a lot. They're very popular and so easy to make." Annie looked proud.

"So, we're all still going to the Sky High Tavern tomorrow night, right?" Landry asked the group. "We have to give Annie a great send-off. I sure wish she wasn't leaving. Oh, and I meant to tell you guys that I'm picking up Ms. Millie from the bus station in Wrigley Springs Saturday at 6pm. She is coming home a day early." She laughed and so did the guys. They all knew that Ms. Millie and Vanessa rarely made it to the finish line where Ms. Millie's visits were concerned.

Adam nodded his head. "Yep. I have my schedule cleared for tomorrow. What time did you want me to pick y'all up? No sense in taking lots of cars. We can just ride together."

Wyatt spoke up, "You can just drop by the Sheriff's Office around 6 and pick me up if that's good for you. I've already told Cora that she'll be in charge until I get back. She'll only call me in case of an emergency. Then, you can drop me back at the Office when we get back to town." Cora Flint was one of Wyatt's deputies.

Adam nodded and looked at Landry, "Wyatt and I will come by to pick the two of you up after I get him. Is that ok?"

"Sure is. We'll be in the lobby so that you don't have to come up."

Adam stood up. "Sounds good. I have to get going since I need to run by the B&B to look at the sink in one of the bathrooms there. I'm hoping it's just a broken seal and I can fix it quickly for her."

Adam's mother, Judith Wilcox, owned Judith's B&B

in town. Adam always tried to repair anything that he could to save his mother money since she had raised him and his sister, Ivy, all by herself after his father had left them when Adam was very young. They hadn't heard from Mr. Wilcox since the day he left.

The others stood up and Annie began gathering coffee mugs and the cookie platter to take to the kitchen. Zep woke up and went back inside, following Annie.

Wyatt said, "Yeah, I have to be going too. I need to stop by the department and check in on some things before I head home for the night."

Landry followed them all inside and closed and locked the sliding glass doors to the balcony. She turned to walk them to the door when somehow her foot got tangled in the drapes and down she went. The others rushed to help her up but she swatted them away. "I'm fine, just clumsy."

She got up and the guys left for the night. Annie had put all of the dishes in the dishwasher and started it.

"I think I am going to bed. For some reason, I'm very tired tonight," Annie told Landry and yawned.

"That's fine. I think I'm going to sit in the den a while and read my book. Our book club has its first meeting the last week of the month and I need to start reading. The book we chose has great reviews and I can't wait to get started on it." Landry smiled and told Annie goodnight.

After checking to make sure everything was locked for the night, Landry went to her bedroom and put on some comfy sweats and socks. She called Zep and the two of them went into the den and settled in to read. Just as she was getting interested in the book, her phone rang. She looked at it and groaned.

"Hi, mother. How are you doing?"

Claire Burke had divorced Landry's father years ago and was now living the life of a socialite, traveling to country after country on the money she'd inherited from her aunt. She rarely had time to talk to Landry.

"I am fine, dear. How are things going there? Please tell me that you have not found another body." Claire would never get over the fact that Landry had found not one but two bodies during her first days in Bobwhite Mountain.

"No, mother, I haven't. Actually, Annie's here visiting me this week. We've enjoyed each other's company so much. I hate to see her leave Saturday morning."

"Oh, Annie. Such a sweet young girl. A little eccentric, but aren't a lot of people these days?" Claire said.

"Where are you, mother? What country, I mean?" Landry asked her globe-trotting mother.

"I am in Italy. You remember the Manoses. They live here and Natalie Manos called and invited me to come stay with them for a while. Her husband had to go to Germany for a conference and she was so lonely. We have had a great time catching up and visiting some Italian tourist spots. I'm really enjoying it." Claire sounded like she truly was having a nice time.

"That's great. I'm sitting on my couch with Zep reading a book that we will be discussing in the book club I started at the bookstore. I cooked dinner earlier for Annie,

Adam and Wyatt and then Annie went to bed since she was so tired from the day we had."

"Who is Wyatt? Of course I know Annie and this Adam that was in your bedroom that time I called." Claire sighed.

"Mother, Adam was just bringing me coffee, since I could hardly move after that horrible woman attacked me on my balcony. Anyway, Wyatt is the sheriff in town. He's also a friend of mine and we all got together for a meal tonight." Landry explained.

"Oh, dear. I have to run. Natalie said that our driver is waiting downstairs to take us to a show we're going to see. I love you, darling. Toodles," Claire said as she hung up the phone.

Landry knew that her mother's inquiries of Landry's life were just Claire being social. She really didn't care what Landry was doing, she just wanted to think that she was being a good mom. Landry loved her mother but had accepted a long time ago that she was never a priority in Claire's life. Even as a young child, it had been her Aunt Tildie that had taken her to social events or fun activities.

She and Zep settled back down and read several chapters of the book. It was very interesting and Landry knew that she loved it already. Finally, when her eyes started drooping and she couldn't focus on the words anymore, she picked up Zep and they went to bed.

Chapter 4

The next morning, after they ate breakfast, Annie told Landry that she was going to spend the day packing up her car in the garage and getting ready to leave early the next morning. Since they were going to the Sky High tonight, Annie wanted to have everything packed before that. She and Landry had planned to use this last night together for a "slumber party" in Landry's room just like they used to have. After they got back from dinner with Wyatt and Adam, they would put on their favorite movie, "St. Elmo's Fire", pop some popcorn and pile up in bed with their pj's to watch the movie and laugh about old times.

Landry told her that was fine, since she was going over to the bookstore today to help Jenna get everything done before Ms. Millie's return to the bookstore on Monday. Even though Landry would pick her up tomorrow at 6 at the bus station in Wrigley Springs, the bookstore was closed on Sunday. Ms. Millie would be there bright and early on Monday morning, however, to let Landry know how she'd failed miserably in Ms. Millie's absence. This was fine with Landry. She and Ms. Millie had a strange relationship. Ms. Millie spoke her mind and did what she wanted to do. Landry nodded and agreed with Ms. Millie. That was mostly because she thought of Ms. Millie as a surrogate aunt now that Aunt Tildie was gone.

Landry had been in the office of the bookstore for about an hour when she heard a customer walk in. Jenna looked up and said, “Hey, Mrs. Dinky. How is Cecil doing? We sure have missed him picking up our mail.”

“He’s as grumpy as ever. I just stopped by to pick up a few books to keep him occupied.” Dinky looked around the bookstore and asked Jenna, “Are you all alone here today?”

“No ma’am. Miss Landry is in the office in the back,” Jenna replied.

Landry walked out of the office and greeted Dinky. “Hello, Dinky. Like Jenna said, we’ve been so concerned about Cecil. We’ve also been concerned about you having to care for him.”

“Oh, I manage. I used to be a nurse and I know what he needs. He likes to read western books and sci-fi. I’m not sure which ones he’s read. Can I just buy a couple of each and, if he’s read them, bring them back and exchange them?” Dinky asked Landry.

“Of course. As a matter of fact, find the ones you think he would like at no charge to you. They will be my get well gift to him. If he’s already read them, still bring them back and we’ll be glad to exchange them for something else.” Landry smiled.

“Oh, how very kind of you. I’ll do just that. I’ll also be sure to tell him they are from you. He loves this bookstore. He and I both still miss Miss Tildie. She was always a great friend to us.”

As Dinky picked out some books for Cecil, Penney Goode came in the door. She lived at Magnolia Place with her mother, Mary Goode. Penney was in college now and was a very responsible young woman.

Jenna looked up and smiled at her friend. "Hey, Penney. How's it going?"

Landry looked at the two friends there together. Both of them had long blonde hair and both were on the thin side. They had been in the same grade in school and had graduated together just this past May. Penney started college this fall at the local Junior College and worked part time at a boutique on Main Street called, "The Elegant Ensemble." Jenna had enrolled in online college courses and made the move from part time to full time at Jasmine Bloom Books. Both girls were very responsible and mature for their age.

Landry looked over at Dinky, who had to use one of the bookstore's wooden step stools to reach the top shelf to get a book for Cecil. Landry smiled to herself and thought about how small of a woman Dinky was.

Penney smiled and said, "Hey, Jenna. I stopped by to see if the copy of *"Jane Eyre"* that I need for my class this semester had come in yet. I just got done with my run and I start my shift at the boutique soon, so I wanted to pick it up if it came in."

"It sure did," Jenna told her. "I have it right here for you. Since you pre-paid, I'll just put it in a bag."

Landry thought of something and said, "Penney, please be very careful when you go for your jogs. Remember, we have a woman missing at the moment. Make sure to watch your surroundings."

As Penney took the bag from Jenna, she said, "Don't worry about me, Landry. I'm very careful to just jog down

Main while there are lots of people around. I also go to the park to jog the perimeter, but only if I see that it's occupied with people all around."

"Good," Landry said. "Until we find out just what happened to Carla, I'll worry about all of us."

Penney waved goodbye and left to drop the book off at home and change clothes before she headed to the boutique.

Dinky walked up to the counter as Penney left and thanked Landry again for the books. She'd chosen two westerns and two sci-fi books for Cecil to read.

Landry couldn't help herself. She asked Dinky, "Is Dinky your nickname? I just think that is such a cute name."

Dinky smiled and said, "Yes, it is. When I was a little girl, I was always the runt of any group of children. Somebody said I was 'a dinky little thing' and it stuck. I'm only four foot eleven, so I guess it's appropriate."

They all laughed and Dinky said goodbye.

"She seems like such a nice person. Don't you ever wonder how she and Cecil got together? I mean, I like Cecil a lot. I know he has a rough exterior but I like to think that he is a teddy bear inside. But, you have to admit, they don't seem like a couple who would click," Jenna told Landry.

"It's amazing sometimes that people who are so different can come to love each other and spend the rest of their lives together," Landry agreed, nodded and went back to the office.

Later, she was putting out some new books that they had just gotten in when the front door swung open and she heard, "Hey, Boss Lady!" Landry smiled at Maisy's greeting.

"Hey, Maisy. Did you have a good day at school today?" Landry asked her.

"Well, that's what I need to talk to you about. See, tryouts for volleyball are today at 4. I was wondering if I could have this afternoon off so that I could be there. The coach has assured me that if I make the team, all practices and games won't start before 6:15pm so that I can still work afternoons here. The coach is the one who asked me to try out. They don't have such good players right now and she's hoping to coerce some of the more athletic kids to try out." Maisy laughed.

"I think that'll be fine, Maisy. We haven't been busy today. I can stay for a little while longer and if we're still slow, we'll just close up early. Does that sound ok to you, Jenna?" Landry asked.

"Sure, Miss Landry. If we happen to get busy, I can handle it by myself." She turned to face Maisy. "I hope you make the team. I know they can surely use you," Jenna told her.

Maisy told them thanks and left to go back to the school. After Maisy was gone, Landry looked at Jenna and said, "Please call me Landry, Jenna. You're a grown woman now and we're friends."

Jenna smiled and nodded her head.

A few minutes later, Annie walked in. She told Landry

that she had gotten all of her things packed up and wanted to walk over and tell Jenna bye before she left tomorrow. They were talking when the door opened and a customer walked in.

"Welcome to the bookstore," Jenna greeted him. Then her eyes got really big.

Landry recognized the customer, even though she had never met him. He was Marston Hayes, a very famous Hollywood actor. He was even more handsome than he appeared in the movies she had seen him in. He was tall with sandy blonde hair, blue eyes and a close cut beard.

He greeted all three of the ladies. "Hi. I'm Marston. I have a vacation home up on the mountain. I need some reference books and your bookstore was highly recommended by my housekeeper." He flashed a gorgeous smile their way.

Landry stepped forward and said, "Hello. I'm Landry Burke and I am the owner. I'm flattered that our store was recommended. Of course, I know who you are. I've seen all of your movies and you are an amazing actor. Now, what can we help you with?"

Marston was staring at Annie and didn't even answer Landry. He pointed to Annie and said, "I think there's something wrong."

They all turned to Annie who was standing there with her mouth open but no sounds were escaping from it. She was holding her throat and Landry noticed she was turning red.

"Annie! What's wrong?" she asked as she ran over to

her friend. Landry noticed the hard candy wrapper on the counter.

"Oh, no! I think she's choking on the candy. Jenna, do you know how to perform the Heimlich maneuver?" Landry frantically asked.

"No. I can do CPR but I never learned about the Heimlich. I'll call 911," Jenna replied.

Marston sprang into action. He got behind Annie and put his arms around her waist, making a fist and putting it against her abdomen. He covered his fist with his other hand and pushed inward and upward. When nothing happened and Annie was still not breathing, he did the same thing again. That time, the piece of candy came flying out of Annie's mouth and onto the floor. She gasped for air and put her hands on her knees to keep her balance."

Landry looked at Marston as he stepped away from Annie. He got in front of her and said, "Are you alright now? Can you breathe okay?"

Annie was staring into his eyes when she answered. "I think so. I mean, yes. I can breathe now. Thank goodness you were here. Thank you for saving my life." Then she hugged the man. Really hugged him and he looked embarrassed.

Landry stepped up and pulled Annie away from him. He smiled at Landry and went back to the counter where Jenna was standing in shock. She had never placed the call to 911 since Marston jumped in to help so fast.

"Wow. You really are a hero. Just like in your movies," she said quietly.

Marston laughed and said, "No, I'm not. It's part of being in show business. They make us take several seminars each year on things like that. Just in case we are taping in a remote location, we need to know how to keep each other safe."

Landry had taken Annie to the back office and sat her down with some water. She walked back up front and asked Marston. "Now that you saved Annie's life, what can we help you with?" She halfway laughed and exhaled a thankful breath at the same time. "I do thank you for helping Annie. She's my best friend and I kind of panicked."

"Ah, not a problem. I'm glad that I happened to be here and knew what to do. What I need are some books on zookeepers. It's for a role I am considering taking and I want to read up on it." He smiled.

Landry found two books that would be perfect for him and he paid for them. Before he left, he walked back and told Annie that he was glad she was ok. Annie just stared at him and finally spoke. "Thanks. You were awesome."

He left the store with his bag of books and Annie walked up front to watch him walk away. "That man is beautiful, Landry. He reminds me of Bradley Cooper, only way more handsome."

"Huh?" Landry asked her. "I mean, Marston is nice looking but, in my book, nobody is more handsome than Bradley."

Annie looked at her like she was nuts and told Jenna goodbye. She left to go back to the apartment.

Later, when Landry left the bookstore for the day, she told Jenna to be sure and lock up when she left. She also told her that if she needed anything at all, to call Magnolia Place or to call her cell.

When Landry got back to her apartment, Annie told her that she had everything packed except what she would need in the morning before she left. She'd already showered and gotten dressed to go out to dinner. She'd also walked Zep and given him fresh food and water. Landry went to get her shower and dress. She made a special note to wear pants…the last time she was at the Sky High in a skirt was a catastrophe. She had noticed that Annie had on jeans and a pretty, frilly top. Annie always looked so good.

Landry got dressed and walked into the living room. Annie was playing catch with Zep and looked up.

"You look amazing! I'm glad you're leaving your hair down tonight. It's so pretty and you always have it pulled up," Annie told her.

"That's because it's so thick and curly. Most of the time, I feel like I'm wearing a mink coat on my back. But tonight is supposed to be cool, so I think it'll be fine." Landry had put on jeans and a lavender sweater set that was thin and would be perfect for tonight. She also wore her ankle boots. She loved boots so much and wore them winter and summer.

They walked down to the lobby to wait on Wyatt and Adam. They didn't have to wait long before the guys pulled up. They hopped into the back of Adam's SUV and headed to the outskirts of town to the Sky High Tavern.

When they arrived, they went up to the small building and told them that they had reservations for the Tavern. The four of them then got on the chair lift that took them to the top of the mountain. Annie was thrilled with their transportation to the restaurant. She and Wyatt rode together in a chair and Landry and Adam were in another one.

Unlike the first time Landry had been here, she jumped out of the chair with ease and didn't fall on top of Adam. They turned around to see Wyatt and Annie laughing as they jumped from the chairlift. It was turning dark now and you could feel the brisk, cool air. Fall was Landry's favorite season of the year and she smiled to herself as she relished in the fact that she now lived in the mountains to enjoy all of the wondrous, vibrant colors of the leaves changing. They were just turning a little now. October was the big show for them.

Landry turned to Wyatt. "I thought of something the other night that I've been meaning to ask you. If the only way to the Sky High Tavern is by chairlift, what would happen if there was a fire or other emergency up here? How would emergency vehicles get here?"

Wyatt smiled and said, "You're one of the most observant and curious people I know, Landry. As a matter of fact, there's a road up the backside of Sky High Mountain that can be used in an emergency. You see, when this place was a tourist attraction, they had an alternate way to get up here. They had an old school bus that carried people up the winding mountain road if they didn't want to take the chairlift. After the Pugh's bought this place to build the Tavern, they only use the road now for deliveries or emergencies. Tell you what, after we eat we can all walk back there to that side of the mountain and I'll show you."

Adam spoke up, "Now, let's go eat. I'm starving." He held the door open for the others.

There was a band playing tonight on the stage with a male lead singer. As Landry looked closer, she recognized Harrison Griffith, the manager of the jewelry store in town. "Hey, I didn't know Harrison sang here. He sounds pretty good."

Annie said, "This is a cool place. The vibe is awesome." She started dancing to the upbeat song the band was playing. She danced all the way to their table as Wyatt and Adam smiled.

Landry told Annie that they also had karaoke here on certain nights and that the locals in town often sang here.

"When I come back for a visit, we'll have to come on a karaoke night. You and I can sing for everybody." She looked at Landry and winked.

"I don't know about all of that. You know I'm a much better dancer than singer, Annie. Don't get me roped into something before you leave tomorrow." Landry looked sad all of a sudden. "I don't want you to leave. I'm going to miss you so much."

Adam spoke up, "Well, just think, Landry. You get to go pick Ms. Millie up tomorrow night from the bus station. When she gets back, you won't have time to mourn Annie's leaving. I'll bet Ms. Millie has hundreds of stories to tell."

Landry made a face at him. "Ha Ha. She's also going to pick apart everything I did at the bookstore while she was gone. She thinks that place belongs to her, not me."

They all laughed and looked at the menu. When they had decided on what they wanted, the waiter took their orders. The guys both got steak meals. Annie got a chef's salad with extra dressing and breadsticks. Landry had a hard time deciding but finally settled on grilled rainbow trout with a loaded potato and broccoli. They all ordered sweet iced tea except for Wyatt who ordered a beer.

They listened to the music while they were waiting on their food. The band was playing 80's songs and Landry was loving it. She wanted to ask Wyatt if there was anything new on Carla Hanson's missing persons case, but didn't want to ruin the fun atmosphere. She'd wait and ask him after they left.

The band stopped for a break and Harrison came over to speak to them. "Hey, guys. Are you enjoying the entertainment tonight?"

Landry nodded her head, "Oh, yeah. I love music from the 80's. I had no idea you sang up here, Harrison. You're very good, by the way."

Harrison dropped his head a little and said, "Thanks, Miss Burke. It's a hobby for me. I was in a garage band in high school and I still like to sing and play guitar when I can."

"Call me Landry, Harrison. We've been enjoying the music greatly." Landry looked up as the waiter brought their food.

"I'll let you guys eat. Thanks for coming tonight." Harrison walked away.

"He seems nice," Annie said. "In fact, everyone I've met in this town seems really nice. I love it here."

Wyatt started cutting his steak and gave Annie a half smile. "Well, you haven't met our mayor yet. He'll ruin our perfect score for you."

Landry and Adam laughed. "Yep. Wyatt's telling the truth. Our mayor isn't a very likable person." Adam said.

Annie leaned her head to one side. "How'd he get elected if nobody likes him?"

Adam answered that. "Because nobody else wanted to be mayor. He was the only one on the ticket at the time. I have a feeling he will not run unopposed in the next election, though."

They all ate and raved about the food. When they were done and had paid the ticket, Landry and Annie stopped by the restroom and Annie told her, "Landry, I know now why you love it in this mountain town. It's very quaint and the people are so welcoming. I don't think I've ever been anywhere like this. Bent Branch is a great place too, but the people just seem so warm and hospitable here. I'm glad you moved here now, although I'll miss you so much when I leave tomorrow."

They walked outside and found Adam and Wyatt. Wyatt took the lead and told them to follow him. He'd borrowed a flashlight from the restaurant and was taking them on a tour of the path to the mountain road before they got on the chairlift to leave. It was a cool night but not cold. The air smelled so fresh and clean to Landry. The Tavern had installed some pathway lights in case an emergency came up and someone had to drive this tiny mountain road. They walked about a half mile and Wyatt told them that it was maybe ten more minutes of walking.

As they were talking amongst themselves, Landry noticed a flower blooming off the side of the road. It was purple and was big. She wondered what kind of flower it could be and walked over to the edge of the road. Adam turned around and said, "Landry, don't go too far off the beaten path. Nobody comes back here much and there might be poison ivy."

Landry said, "Oh, I didn't think about that." She started back onto the road but didn't make it.

One minute she was there talking to Adam and the next she was screaming and disappearing into the ground.

Adam shouted, "Wyatt! Come help!" Then he ran back to where Landry had fallen. He stopped in his tracks when he noticed the huge hole in the ground. He bent down on his hands and knees and called, "Landry! Landry, are you alright?!"

Wyatt and Annie came running up and Adam stopped them before they fell into the hole. He told Wyatt what happened and Wyatt said, "I bet you this is an old well from when this was a tourist attraction years ago. They covered the things up but it has been so long now that it probably cracked and broke when Landry stepped on it."

They all kept yelling for Landry to make sure she was

alright and hadn't broken her leg or worse during the fall. Annie was crying and yelling for Landry. No answer.

They all stopped yelling at the same time and finally heard her. "Wyatt!" was all she said.

"Yes, Landry, I'm here. Are you alright? Are you hurt?" Wyatt yelled.

"I'm not hurt. Wyatt, Carla Hanson isn't missing anymore."

"What? What are you saying, Landry?" Wyatt sounded confused.

"I found her. She's dead and she's lying in front of me. Get. Me. Out. Now. Wyatt."

Chapter 5

Landry stood there, shaking. Her breathing was so rapid that she couldn't even get air in. She started doing her breathing exercises for her anxiety but all she could think of was the putrid air she smelled. Carla's short brown hair was matted with blood. Her eyes were still open and Landry couldn't stop staring at them. She twisted her ring around and around her finger. This was another coping mechanism. None of them seemed to be working. She felt like she was going to pass out.

Suddenly, there was a light shining down from the opening at the top. Adam had the flashlight that Wyatt had borrowed and was shining it down. Landry looked up and Adam had never been so glad to see those bright green eyes looking at him.

"Landry, it's going to be alright," Adam said calmly in his deep voice. "Wyatt has run back to the Tavern to call the Sheriff's Department since his cell wouldn't pick up a signal here. He's getting everybody out here as fast as they can come. Landry, back off as far away as you can from Carla's body. Don't disturb the scene any more than you have to. Keep doing your breathing exercises."

Landry looked up at him, "Adam, please don't leave me. Please stay here with me until they get me out. I'm so scared of what else might be down here besides me and Carla. I mean, a body is bad enough but–" Her words drifted off.

"I would not ever leave you, Landry. Annie is here, too. We're both staying right here until they get you out of there. Just keep talking to us and stay as far away from the body as you can. It'll be alright in just a little while." Adam was so scared for her that he could hardly think but he knew he had to remain calm and collected for both her and Annie, who was over by a tree losing her dinner right now.

Landry was spinning her ring and praying. He heard her asking the Lord to please get her out of there soon. That melted his heart. He wished it was him down there instead of her.

Annie walked back up and knelt down to talk to Landry. "Hey, Lan. At least you look good tonight. Ya never know, there might be a hunk coming to rescue you."

Adam looked at Annie like she was completely crazy and shook his head a little. "That's what you got?" he said to her in a low voice. "That's what you thought would be helpful in this situation?"

Annie shrugged. "I've never been in this situation before. I'm doing my best." She ran her fingers through her blue hair.

Landry yelled, "I can hear you both, you know. Wow, this night has turned into dinner and a show." She said sarcastically.

Wyatt came running back up and told them that help would be here soon. He bent down and said, "Hey, Red. Are you really ok physically? You aren't bleeding or anything or you?"

"No. At least not that I can tell. Wyatt, it stinks down

here. I want to throw up but I don't want to make this any worse. Carla's head has been bashed in. She looks like she has bruises on her neck, too. Who would do something like this? I feel like I am going to pass out." Landry's voice was getting weaker.

"Nope. You are not going to pass out. You have to stay with me, Landry. It won't be long until we'll get you out of there." He looked at Adam and put his index finger to his mouth. Then he said, "Tell ya what, Red. If you'll just stay awake and not pass out, when you get back up here, I'll give you a kiss like you've never experienced."

Adam jumped up and started to say something to Wyatt but Wyatt waved his hand and said quietly, "It's the shock value, Adam. We don't need her to pass out right now. She might have hit her head and has a concussion. Also, if she passes out, she might fall face first into mud and suffocate. Just play along."

They looked back down into the hole. Wyatt punched Adam on the arm. "Look."

Landry was standing up straight and her mouth was dropped open. Her eyes were wide open and she looked like she was offended and furious.

"Wyatt Collins, that is just rude. Don't try to make a play for me when I'm in a hole, with a dead woman and heaven only knows what else. How could you be so crass?!"

Wyatt stood up and smiled at Adam. "See? I told you it'd work. Now, I hear the trucks coming up the mountain. I'm going to show them where we are."

He walked by Annie and she had a crazy looking face on her and said, "You don't play fair, Wyatt. I hope you know she's going to have your hide for that."

Wyatt just smiled and started running down the road to meet the emergency vehicles.

Adam and Annie kept talking to Landry until help arrived. They then stepped back out of the way so that the emergency workers could get her out.

As that was happening, Wyatt came over and looked at Adam. "Can you and Annie run back to the Tavern and see if they have any dry clothes there for Landry to put on when she's out of the well? You can tell the Pugh's what's going on, but be discreet and don't let any of the others there hear you. I'm pretty sure that Lucy Pugh keeps extra clothes here in case they get stuck up here. There's water in the bottom of the well, and I know Landry will be freezing once we get her up here."

They nodded started walking back to the tavern to see what they could find.

About that time, one of Wyatt's deputies called out for him and Wyatt looked back to see the top of Landry's head coming up out of the well. He ran over to her.

She got on solid ground and fell into him, crying and shaking uncontrollably. Everything hit her at once and she could hardly breathe. Wyatt hugged her and tried to calm her down. All of a sudden, she swung at him and hit him on the head.

"Hey! What are you doing? I got you out of that nasty hole in the ground." Wyatt rubbed his arm.

"I cannot believe you said that to me in front of Adam and Annie. About the kiss. What were you thinking? Now, they probably think we're seeing each other or something." Landry was furious.

"No, they don't. I did that to shock you into being angry so that you wouldn't pass out on me until I could get you out." Wyatt half smiled at her. "But, I can give you that kiss if you want?"

She told him she would pass and he threw his head back and laughed. "I know you like Adam and I think that's great. He likes you, too, you know." Wyatt said to her.

She just stared at him. He looked over her shoulder and said, "Here's Adam and Annie now. I sent them to find you some dry clothes. You can go to the restroom right inside the front door of the Tavern and change. Come back here after you're done. Take Annie with you just in case you feel dizzy or something from being in the well."

She thanked him as he walked back to the well to check on the progress of getting Carla's body out of there. They had the coroner, the forensics team and lots of equipment that they'd brought up the mountain.

She and Annie went to the restroom so that Landry could change clothes. Lucy brought them each a coffee before they started back to the well. Landry was so grateful since she was still shaking even after she had put the dry sweatpants, shirt, socks and jacket on that Lucy had lent her. She even had to take her boots off and throw them away. They would be ruined from standing in all the muck in the well. Lucy had given her some sneakers to wear.

They were a little big on her but with the socks on, they were fine.

By the time they got back to the well, Carla's body had been removed and was on the way to Margie Hammond's lab. Margie was the coroner. The deputies and firemen that had responded to the call had put up barriers around the open well until they had someone come back tomorrow to close it completely.

Wyatt walked up to the three of them and said, "Why don't you three come walk with me to my vehicle right down the road. One of my deputies brought it here for me. I will drive you back to Adam's car at the bottom so that you don't have to take the chairlift down. Then, I have to go do the absolute worst part of my job."

Landry's eyes got big. "Oh, Wyatt. I forgot about that. That has to be so hard to do."

"It's awful. Especially to hear that guttural sound of the scream that comes from deep down in a mother's soul when she finds out that her child's gone. Carla's parents live over in Wrigley Springs and I want them to hear this from me before word gets out." Wyatt dropped his head and walked in front of the others to the car.

After Wyatt dropped them at the car, Adam turned on the heat for Landry. She was still shaking but her breathing had gotten better. They rode in silence most of the way home until Landry's phone beeped and she saw that she had a missed call from when her cell didn't work on the mountain.

She checked it and sat up straight. She read it again

and told Adam, "Adam, it's from Jenna's mom, Mrs. Shipman. She said that Jenna hasn't come home from work. This message was sent a couple of hours ago. The bookstore closes at 7pm. Jenna should have been home a long time ago."

Adam glanced over at her. "Landry, Jenna is a grown woman now. She probably met some of her friends after work and lost track of time. Call Mrs. Shipman back. Jenna is probably in bed by now."

Landry called Mrs. Shipman only to find out that Jenna was still not home. Mrs. Shipman said that her husband was out of town with work and they only had his car and the one Jenna drove. She said that Jenna had promised to be home right after work so that her Mom could go pick up some things for the younger kids at the grocery store while Jenna watched them for her. Mrs. Shipman was worried sick. Landry told her to try to calm down and she would see what she could find out.

They were turning down Main Street then, and Landry told Adam to go straight to the bookstore. When they got to the front door, Landry had a confused look on her face.

"What is it, Lan?" Annie asked.

"The door is locked but this sign that's here is only used when one of us is here alone and has to go to the restroom or receive deliveries at the back door for a few minutes." She got out her key and unlocked the door. "Also, the blinds are still up and we always put those down when we're closed and put the closed sign up. Look, even the lights are still on in here and that candle has burnt almost all the way down." Landry looked worried and turned to Adam.

"I'm going to check the Children's Room to make sure there's nobody there. Will you please go check the back office for me?" she asked him.

Adam nodded and went towards the back of the store. Landry and Annie went into the Children's Room, a separate room for the kids to read, play and watch movies. It had been a small storage room before they remodeled it. Landry turned on the overhead light and saw that nobody was in there. She and Annie were just leaving the room when Landry heard Adam shout her name.

She ran to the back office and stopped in her tracks. The back door was wide open and the night air was seeping in.

"Was it open like this when you walked in here?" She looked at Adam.

"Yes. Completely open. I need you to step out the door with me." He motioned for her to follow him.

When they got outside, Landry saw that there was only one small car in the lot. It was Jenna's car.

Landry started shaking and twisting her ring. She had tears in her eyes and looked at Adam. "Oh no. Carla was missing and we found her body tonight. Now, Jenna's missing. Adam, please tell me this is a dream. Not Jenna. She is just starting to live her life after high school. Not Jenna!" Landry screamed into the night.

Adam told Annie to get Landry back inside while he called Wyatt. He only hoped that Wyatt was done with the terrible task of telling Carla's parents about her when he called.

Wyatt picked up right away. He told Adam that he just got back to the Sheriff's Office. Adam told him about Jenna being missing.

"I'm on my way. Stay there. Don't touch anything." Wyatt slammed the phone down.

He was there in a matter of minutes. He walked through the bookstore and listened to everything they told him. "Please give me Mrs. Shipman's number, Landry. I want to call her and let her know what we've found so far."

He then called his office and told them to send someone to dust for prints and take some pictures. He walked out to Jenna's car and noticed that it was still locked up. Nothing looked disturbed inside the vehicle. He walked back inside and called Mrs. Shipman before the rest of his crew got there.

"Not my baby girl. Oh no." Mrs. Shipman was crying.

"We're going to find her. I need you to stay calm for me. We'll be by in the morning to get some pictures of Jenna so that we can put up fliers and put her picture on TV. I'm sure she's still in town somewhere, Mrs. Shipman. We won't stop until we find her. We'll take her car down to the department and look it over. Nothing looks disturbed, though. I'll get it to you as soon as we're done."

Wyatt hung up the phone and Landry called out to him to come to the back office. She was pulling up the security camera footage on the office computer. "Remember a few months back when I had security cameras installed at

Magnolia Place after Fred's murder? I also had them installed here at the bookstore. We should be able to see who came in before Jenna went missing."

Wyatt's eyes got big. "That's amazing, Landry. Pull it up, please."

She did and they watched it. It showed Jenna at the counter around the time Landry had left to go get ready to go to Sky High Tavern. Several people came in and left after that. Nothing unusual that they could see. Landry knew most of the customers and they all seemed to act perfectly normal and Jenna didn't seem concerned at all. Then, around 6:30pm, they saw Jenna look towards the back office and say something. The cameras didn't have audio, so they didn't know what she said exactly but it looked like to Wyatt that she said, 'just a minute'."

Jenna then went to the front door, locked it and put the "be right back" sign on the door. She went straight back to the office. There wasn't a camera in the small office so they couldn't see who was there or what they said. Landry assumed that it was a delivery person who rang the bell at the back door to let Jenna know there was a delivery.

"The more I think about that, Wyatt, we don't have deliveries that late at night. In fact, during the winter months, we close up at 5pm. We stay open until 7pm now since the weather's still good. We never schedule deliveries that late. Jenna may have thought it was a delivery truck that was running late, I guess." Landry had a confused look on her face.

Wyatt said, "Or, when she went to answer the door and

looked out of the peephole, she may have recognized the person and felt safe opening the door to them. At least we have a timeframe of when she was taken. Good job putting the cameras in, Landry. Where is the second one you mentioned?"

"It's in the Children's Room for the peace of mind of their parents. I already checked that footage and nobody went in there after I left yesterday," Landry told him.

Wyatt nodded at her as his deputies and crew walked in. He started directing them and telling them what he needed them to do. He looked at Landry, Adam and Annie.

"Sorry, guys. I really need you to leave now. Landry, I'll lock up tight when we're done here. In fact, I might still be here when you open in the morning. What a night," Wyatt said to them.

"Do you think Jenna's disappearance is connected to Carla's?" Annie asked Wyatt.

"We haven't had a kidnapping here since I've been the Sheriff. That's years. I can't help but think the two are related. We have to find Jenna fast. Whoever killed Carla is still out there and I don't like the fact that Jenna could be with that kind of person." He looked at Landry. "Do not, and I mean do not, let anyone be here at the store by themselves. That includes you and Ms. Millie. Always have two people here. Whoever took Jenna took her from this store. Be more careful than you've ever been. Got it?"

"Got it. I'll close the store before I let any of us be here alone. Please, Wyatt, find Jenna and get her back to her Momma. Jenna's family isn't wealthy by any means, but their family is their world." Landry turned to leave. "And, thank you for everything you are doing. I know this is hard for you and I appreciate your dedication."

She and Annie walked out while Adam held the door for them. They started to walk across the road to Magnolia Place and he called out, "Wait up, ladies. I'll walk you to the door of your apartment. I'm not taking any chances tonight."

After he left, Landry locked up. She changed Zep's potty pads and put down fresh water and food. She had him in her arms and was loving on him when Annie came back in the room from the bathroom.

"Go get a shower, Landry. A hot one. Put on your pj's and get in bed. I'll grab my shower in the hall bathroom and do the same. Zep will be done eating by then and we can lie down. I know we were going to watch a movie tonight, but we can just talk and get some sleep if you want to. It's fine with me. Please take your anxiety medicine, too. This has been an awful night for you." Annie walked up to her and hugged her. "I'm praying that Wyatt finds Jenna soon. I know he won't stop until he does."

"So do I. I just don't want him to find her in the same shape as Carla was in." Landry got tears in her eyes. "Oh, Annie. I'm going to miss you so much. I wish you could stay."

Annie smiled, "You have no idea how much I wish I could but I have to get back and run the bakery. I'll visit again soon, though. I promise."

Landry sighed, "I'll do everything you asked me to but

I have to call Maisy first. She works on Saturdays now since Jenna went full time and I need to tell her a couple of things."

Landry dialed Maisy's home number and her Mom, Sybil, picked up.

"Hello, Sybil. This is Landry. We've had some things happen tonight and I need to tell you about them."

Landry proceeded to tell Sybil about Carla's death and also Jenna's disappearance.

"I'll open the bookstore at 10am tomorrow. Please don't bring Maisy to work until then. We have to meet in front before I open up. In no way, shape or form can we have just one person in the bookstore until all of this is solved. Also, I know Maisy walks from school in the afternoons most of the time to come to work. Please don't let her walk anywhere alone right now. If you can't pick her up and bring her, just let me know ahead of time and I'll find someone to pick her up or I'll find someone else to work for her that day," Landry pleaded with her.

"Oh my goodness. This is awful. I'll bring her and pick her up every day until this is solved. If I can't pick her up one day, Ms. Millie always brings her home after they close during the weekdays." Sybil told her. "And, don't worry. I won't let Maisy walk anywhere alone. She's going to be so upset about Jenna. Do they have any idea where she could be?"

"I'm afraid not. I know Maisy's going to be upset and confused and that's why I wanted to tell you the details and let you tell her. Thanks, Sybil. I'll see you both at 10 in the morning." Landry hung up.

Chapter 6

After they both got showers, they settled into Landry's bed for their sleepover. Zep was laying in between the two of them and was already snoring.

Annie looked at Zep but she was talking to Landry. "So, what's up with you and Adam? I mean, it's very obvious that he really likes you. Where do the two of you stand right now?"

"After the night I've had, you're gonna ask me that question? I was trapped with a woman's body in a well filled with disgusting smelling gunk and then I found out that Jenna's missing and you want to know about me and Adam?" Landry laughed. "Same old Annie…ignore anything that might upset Landry."

"Well, I figure you've had enough of murderous talk tonight. Just thought I'd lighten the mood," Annie said defensively.

"I know." Landry looked properly scolded. "I guess I'm still on edge from tonight. To answer your question, I'm not really sure where Adam and I are at. We're very good friends and I do like him a lot. He's such a gentleman and he does love his momma." They both laughed at that.

"Yep, that's a requirement in the south. If a man doesn't love and treat his momma right, you know he won't treat you right." Annie pulled her pillow up and laughed again.

"We've never had any conversation other than as

friends. I'm not sure where we're headed. Or, if we're headed anywhere other than friendship. I guess we'll wait and see." Landry looked like she was getting sleepy.

"What about Wyatt?" Annie couldn't resist asking about him. "He seems a little smitten with you, too."

Landry didn't hesitate. "Oh, he and I are just friends. I like Wyatt…I even love him as a friend. But, that's all. He just likes to tease me like he would a sister."

"Uh-huh. A sister." Annie yawned. "Well, we better get to sleep. I have to drive home tomorrow and you have to work at the bookstore and then pick up the infamous Ms. Millie. I sure wish I could stay to meet her."

"Ugggh. Ms. Millie. I have to tell her about all of this stuff going on in town. She's going to flip out and figure out some way to make it my fault. Yep. Better get some shuteye." Landry turned over and flipped the light off. She was snoring lightly in just a few minutes.

When her alarm went off the next morning, Landry saw that Annie wasn't in the room. She sat straight up in bed and panicked for a minute until she got a whiff of something. Coffee. Annie must be making coffee. She and Zep got up and went into the kitchen. There was Annie, sitting at the table, drinking her coffee and crying like a baby.

Landry walked over and hugged her. "You scared me for a second. I woke up and you were gone. I thought someone had snatched you in the middle of the night." She walked over to pour herself a cup of coffee. "What's wrong, Annie?"

"Nothing. I'm just sad that I'm leaving in a couple of hours to go home. I wish I could stay here with you. Landry, promise me you're going to be careful when I'm gone. I know how you like to get involved in things like this. I can't lose my best friend. Please, just promise me." Annie looked at Landry with a very serious look on her face.

"I promise. I'll be extra careful. Look, Annie, this has shaken me up, too. I'm so worried about Jenna. I'll pass out fliers and help look for her with lots of other people around but I won't go anywhere by myself unless I know it's somewhere safe. I don't want you to go, either. We didn't have enough time together. It was so much easier when we lived in the same town and saw each other every day." Landry sighed and took a sip of her coffee.

"It sure was." Annie agreed. "Oh well, I have to start getting ready to leave. It's about a five hour trip and I want to stop in and check on the bakery before I go to my house to make sure everything's ready for Monday."

Landry's phone rang and she saw it was Wyatt. She grabbed it up and answered it with, "Did you find her? Did you find Jenna?"

"Not yet, Landry. I'm sorry. I wish I could tell you 'yeah', but not yet. I wanted to let you know that I locked everything up at the bookstore about 3am when we finally got done. We didn't find anything that was helpful. Of course, there are hundreds of prints in there because it's a business that's frequented by lots of people. We didn't even see any signs of a struggle in the back parking lot. I'm going to do a press conference in about an hour letting everybody know that we found Carla's body and that Jenna is now missing. I just hung up with Mrs. Shipman and she has the photos ready for us for the fliers. A deputy is on the way there now. As soon as he's back, we'll make the flier on the computer here and print out as many as we can before the presser. We'll distribute them there and then make more for people to put up in businesses and such. I know that most people in town know Jenna but just in case, I want her picture out to as many people as possible. Look, I'm going to be busy today and into the night. I've gotten some information already that might be helpful in Carla's case and I hope to gather more today. I know you have to pick up Ms. Millie tonight, so why don't you, Adam and I meet at my house after church tomorrow? I can throw some steaks on the grill and fill you both in at the same time with what I know."

"That sounds good. I'll be speaking with Adam today before I go to pick up Ms. Millie. Judith fell in her garden and has a sprained ankle so he's going to help out at the B&B today. I'll let him know about coming to your house after church tomorrow," Landry told him.

"Okay. I'll see you guys at church and after we get away from Ms. Millie, we can follow each other to my house. You know that woman is going to be questioning us all about what's gone on since she's been gone." Wyatt laughed. "Oh and Landry, if you hear anything while you're at the bookstore today that might help with the cases, please keep it to yourself until we speak. The less people that know what information we have, the better."

"Will do." Landry hung up and looked at Annie.

"Why don't we go to the diner and eat some breakfast before you leave and I have to be at the bookstore? We can take Zep for a little walk before we go."

"Sounds good to me. I'm going to get dressed." Annie said.

While they were on their walk with Zep, they were both looking suspiciously at everyone they saw. Both were wondering if that person could be a kidnapper or killer.

After they got back to the apartment and dropped Zep off, they headed back to the lobby. Orvis wasn't due to report for his lobby assistant position until 9 on weekends, but he was already there at the desk.

"Hey, Orvis. Why are you here so early?" Landry asked.

"Hey, Landry. I woke up and couldn't go back to sleep, so I decided I might as well go ahead and come down here." He nodded at Annie.

"Oh," Landry said, "I'm sorry. Orvis, this is Annie, my best friend. Annie, this is Orvis. He works in the lobby on the weekends."

They told each other hello and then Landry told Orvis about Carla and Jenna. He was shocked.

"Oh no. Jenna is so young, Landry. I pray they find her soon."

"Everyone does, Orvis. Annie and I are going to the diner for breakfast and then I'll be going to the bookstore.

Maisy's mom is dropping her off at 10 and she and I will work together today. Try to keep an eye out if you can." Landry told him.

"Oh, no problem. If you need anything, just call me and I'll come right over," Orvis said.

Landry told him she would and she and Annie left. When they got to the diner, they grabbed a booth and ordered coffee. After the coffee came, they both ordered the same thing…the breakfast platter. It came with bacon, sausage, eggs, grits and a biscuit. They were both hungry after the night they had.

Several people greeted them as they came in. Jason Boyd, who lived at Magnolia Place and was a Pharmacy Tech, rode his bicycle to the diner and left it outside. He told them hello and went to sit at the counter. A few minutes later, Troy and Deidre Mills, who also lived in the building, stopped to say hello. Troy had just opened a dental practice in town and was in the process of building up his client base after the previous dentist retired. Deidra was a receptionist at a local doctor's office. They had moved to Bobwhite Mountain after Troy graduated from dental school. He had relatives in town that had told him about the other dentist retiring. Landry and Annie spoke to all of them and then the waitress brought their food out.

As they were eating, Landry looked out of the window by their booth and moaned.

"What is it?" Annie asked as she looked out to see what had gotten Landry upset.

"Nothing. See that woman there in the bright lavender

dress? That's Pam. She's a local real estate agent and Adam's ex. She grates on my nerves," Landry seethed.

Annie smiled. "See, there is more to you and Adam than just friends. I knew it," she said smugly.

"Stop it, Annie. It's not that. It's just that everybody I have heard talk about Pam says the same thing. She is spoiled, possessive and a narcissist. Even Lisa can't stand her and Lisa likes everybody. Anyway, she's gone now." Landry went back to eating.

They finished up their breakfast and went back to Magnolia Place. Annie got the rest of her things together and took them down to her car in the garage. She went back up to be sure she had everything and Zep ran up to her. She sat down on the sofa and he jumped into her lap and gave her kisses.

"Well, that's a big improvement over the first time you two met." Landry smiled. "I do believe Zep is going to miss you almost as much as I am."

"I'm going to miss him, too. He's grown on me," Annie laughed.

Zep jumped down and stood in front of her. He yipped and whined like he knew she was leaving them. He turned around and around in circles, which Landry knew meant that he was nervous and upset. She walked over and picked him up. "I'll take him with us to the garage so that he can see you leave. That way, he'll know that you aren't coming back soon."

They went downstairs and into the garage. They both stood there, with Landry holding Zep in her arms. Both of them had tears in their eyes.

"Love you, Tiny Dancer." Annie called Landry by the childhood name she had given her since Landry was always dancing around everywhere.

"I love you, too, Tink." Landry had given Annie this name because she floated everywhere she went like she was walking on clouds.

Annie got in her car and put on her seatbelt. She rolled her window down and told Landry that she would be back soon. "As soon as the bakery lets me." She laughed. "And, stay away from Marston until I get back. I don't want him falling for you before I at least get a chance."

Landry and Zep stood there until Annie was out of the garage and on the way back to Bent Branch. Zep started whining and Landry rubbed his head and said, "Me too, Zep. Me, too."

She took him back to the apartment and got him settled in. She put down new pads for him, gave him fresh water and food, turned on the TV to the game show channel that he liked to listen to when she was out, and put him down some treats for the day. She then went and washed her hands, grabbed her purse and went to the lobby. She waited there and talked to Orvis until she saw Maisy's mom, Sybil, drop Maisy off for work. She ran across the street to meet them.

Sybil looked at her hopefully. "Any word on Jenna?"

"No, I'm afraid not," Landry told her, then walked over to Maisy and put her arms around her. "I'm sorry, Maisy. I know how much you like Jenna. They're going to find her."

Maisy just nodded her head. Landry had never seen her sad like this before. "You know, Maisy, I have a lot to do today before I pick up Ms. Millie tonight. If you want to go back home with your Mom, we can close the store for today."

"Oh no, Boss Lady, I want to work today. It'll help me to have something to do. I'm just so worried about Jenna, ya know?" Maisy said to Landry.

"I do. So am I. Let's go inside and see what we need to do." Landry waved goodbye to Sybil and unlocked the door. They walked in and saw that the deputies had kind of made a mess last night.

"Well, I guess we do have lots to keep us busy today." Landry smiled at Maisy.

They got things cleaned up and organized. They had several customers that day, most of whom asked about Jenna. Wyatt had given his press conference that morning and the town was buzzing about Carla's death and Jenna's disappearance. Landry saw lots of people with fliers in their hands going into all the businesses to put them in the front windows. Jasmine Bloom had a flier in each of their windows and one in a frame on the front desk. Maisy had also gotten a stack of them from a customer so that she could put one in every bag of a person who bought anything there. Landry had called Orivs and he ran over to get one to put in the window and on the door of Magnolia Place. At least they felt like they were doing something to help bring Jenna home.

Landry had Maisy call her Mom at 3pm and ask her to come pick her up. Landry had to get ready to go pick up Ms. Millie and they hadn't had a customer come in the store for over an hour. When Sybil got there to pick up Maisy, Landry locked the front door and ran over to Magnolia Place before Sybil pulled off to leave. Orvis met her at the door and opened it for her.

Landry sighed as she said to Orvis, "This is crazy. I hate that I have to be watched like a toddler just walking across the street from the bookstore to the apartment building. I hope we find Carla's killer and bring Jenna home soon."

Orvis agreed with her and she walked towards the elevator to go up and get ready to go to Wrigley Springs. She heard someone behind her calling her name. She turned around and saw Adam.

"Hey." She smiled at him. "What are you doing here? I thought you were at the B&B all day today."

Adam smiled back and walked towards her. "I am. I had a few minutes before I had to get things ready for dinner so I told Mom to stay in bed and rest until I got back. I thought I would come take Zep for a walk, since I don't want you walking him by yourself right now."

They got on the elevator and Landry said, "Thanks. That would be great. I know he misses his walks and he needs to get some energy out."

They walked into her apartment and there was Zep in the living room waiting. Landry knew he must be so ready to go walk since he usually was asleep on the couch in the den when she dropped in during the day to check on him. He started wagging his tail so fast that it looked like a helicopter blade going around. He was whining and spinning around in circles. Adam started laughing, got his leash and said they were going to go.

"I'm going to make myself a bagel with cream cheese and some coffee to eat before I get dressed. Do you want one?" Landry asked Adam as she started in the kitchen.

"Thanks, but no. I have eaten way too much today already. Mom has so many different things to snack on at the B&B. Besides, I want to give this little guy as long of a walk as I can before I head back to Mom's." Adam reached down and picked Zep up to take him to the elevator.

Landry told them goodbye and then ate her bagel. She put on a pair of jeans, a sweatshirt and her boots. The temperature was supposed to drop some tonight. She changed Zep's potty pads, gave him fresh water. She saw that his food bowl was still half full, which wasn't unusual. He only weighed 8 pounds and he was a smart dog. He only ate what filled him up and left the rest until later. She then sat down on the sofa to wait until Adam got back before she left.

Adam walked her down to the garage and told her to be careful on the way to Wrigley Springs by herself. She told him that she would and that she was going to park her car right near where the bus arrived so she could help Ms. Millie with her bags. They waved goodbye and she drove away.

Chapter 7

The ride to Wrigley Springs went great. There was hardly any traffic on the roads. It was starting to get dark and Landry had listened to her 80's music the entire way there. She was disappointed to see that all of the parking spaces up front were already taken. She had to pull around the back and park in the lot there. Landry lowered her window a little so she could hear the bus pull in. She and all of the other people parked in the lot got out and walked to the front to meet the bus. Landry ran up to Ms. Millie and hugged her. "Hey. I sure have missed you. How was the bus ride back?" Landry asked.

"You don't want to know. I had a lady with a screaming baby sitting next to me and a man behind me who appeared to be nine feet tall, since his knees stayed on my back the entire trip."

They walked towards the luggage area of the bus and Ms. Millie continued. "Then, the girl sitting next to him stayed on her phone the whole time and even though she had headphones on, she laughed and talked so loud to the other person that I now know the complete life story of that girl on the bus. If I wanted to assume her identity, I would have no problem at all. Kids these days are so ignorant when it comes to protecting themselves."

Everyone else got their luggage before Ms. Millie. Landry was praying that they hadn't lost her luggage. That would tip Ms. Millie right over the edge. The porter finally handed them the luggage, which seemed to have had another suitcase added to it since Landry had put her on the bus to go to Mississippi. Landry grabbed the largest one and a duffle bag. Ms. Millie got the smaller one and a travel case.

As they headed towards the car, Ms. Millie continued with her diatribe. Landry was wondering what in the world she was thinking by asking how the bus ride went. "The absolute worst thing about the trip was that a man in the back of the bus seemed to have stomach issues. He was continuously back and forth to that little bathroom. The whole bus stunk so bad that I thought I was going to pass out. Horrible bus ride. Just horrible."

Landry shook her head and said, "I still think you would enjoy your trips better if you took a plane. It would be so much more comfortable."

At that moment, the large suitcase Landry was carrying burst open. All of Ms. Millie's clothes spilled out onto the concrete and Landry's mouth dropped open.

"Well, if this isn't just perfect. Now you have dumped my unmentionables onto the oily bus station parking lot. Right out here in the open for everybody to ogle. Put that suitcase down, child and help me get these things back in there." Ms. Millie was beside herself as a nice young man stopped and bent down to help them pick the things up.

"Stop it, you pervert," Ms. Millie yelled at him. "Why would you want to touch an old lady's undergarments? Some people are just sick in the head."

The young man jerked his hand back up and stood up

straight. "I was only trying to help. Get your own things up, you nasty woman." He turned and walked away fast.

Not fast enough for Ms. Millie, though. She jumped up and took off after him. Landry left the suitcase and clothes and went running after her. She caught up with her just as Ms. Millie was about to bop the young man in the head and give him what for. Landry grabbed her hand and dragged her back to the suitcase as the man got in his car and left.

"You can't be doing that, Ms. Millie. You never know what some people might be capable of. You're going to have to learn to let things go in this day and time. Some people, especially strangers, don't know how to be as well-mannered as you. Besides, I have lots of news to tell you about things in Bobwhite Mountain and some of it's going to shock and upset you. Let's get this stuff in the car and head home," Landry told her.

When they finally got themselves and everything else in the car and locked the doors as she had promised Adam, Landry said, "I'm so sorry, Ms. Millie. I guess it wasn't fastened completely." "I'll take the clothes to my apartment and wash them for you when we get back home."

Ms. Millie had an appalled look on her face. "I don't think so. Nobody is going to wash my unmentionables but me. Just get me home in one piece, please."

Landry sighed and said, "Yes, ma'am." She started them on the road home.

She was in the process of updating Ms. Millie on everything that had happened in Bobwhite Mountain while she was away. When she got to the part about falling in the well and finding Carla's body, Ms. Millie interrupted her.

"I can't believe you found another body. What is wrong with you, child? Nobody finds bodies like that. I am, however, grateful that you weren't hurt when you fell and I'm even more grateful that you decided to find her body while I was still in Mississippi. Maybe you aren't trying to kill me by giving me a heart attack after all," Ms. Millie conceded.

"I told you that I'm not trying to get you killed. It's just a misfortunate string of events that occurred. Anyway, that's not the worst of it," Landry told her.

"There is something worse than you finding a dead woman in a well after she had been kidnapped?" Ms. Millie looked shocked.

"Yes." Landry braced herself for the reaction she was about to get. "Ms. Millie, when we got back to town that night we discovered Jenna had been kidnapped."

Ms. Millie didn't say anything for a few seconds and Landry wondered if she had actually heard her. Then she said something.

"It cannot be. It just cannot be. That child is one of the sweetest girls I have ever known. I feel like she's one of my own. Landry, we have to find her. No matter what, we have to find Jenna." Ms. Millie wiped her eyes and Landry could hear the emotion in her voice.

"We've been searching everywhere. I'm so sorry I had to tell you, but I knew when we got back to town you would hear about it from somebody else. There are posters and fliers all over town with her picture on them," Landry said quietly.

They were traveling down the long, lonely country road back into Bobwhite Mountain when all of a sudden, the Bug started to sputter and then shut down completely.

"What in the world?" Landry said and tried to crank it back up with no avail.

"Did you check the gas hand before you left to come get me?" Ms. Millie asked.

"Of course I did. I even filled up the gas tank yesterday morning since I knew I'd be coming to pick you up. I don't understand it." Landry looked confused and laid her head back on the seat and sighed.

"See that wooden fence through the woods there?" She asked Ms. Millie. "That's the fence to the lower pasture at the farm. I'm going to have to jump that fence and walk through the pasture to the gate. Then I'll walk up the hill to the house and get help."

Steve and Denise Wilcox, Lisa's parents, had bought the working farm from Landry's Aunt Tildie when she sold it. Landry had spent many summers in her youth there and knew that this was the fence for the pasture. She also knew that her cell phone didn't work on this road until she got closer to Bobwhite Mountain, so jumping the fence was her only choice.

"Ms. Millie, you stay here in the car and lock the doors. I'll be back as soon as I get Steve to bring me and some gas back here."

Ms. Millie slowly turned her head and looked at Landry. She spoke in a clipped, hushed tone. "You would like that, wouldn't you? I should have known."

"What? What in the world are you talking about?" Landry made a questioning face.

"You just told me that there's a kidnapper and murderer on the loose in this area. You want me to stay here, in this toy car that two grown men could pick up and haul away with me in it. You want me to be a sitting duck for a criminal. I'm so disappointed. I thought you'd changed your ways about me." Ms. Millie undid her seatbelt.

Landry looked at her like she had two heads. "You have lost your mind. Ms. Millie, you have on a nice skirt and top and I know those are new suede shoes you are wearing. You can't jump the fence and walk through a pasture. Don't be ridiculous."

"If you go, I go. End of discussion. Now, get out so we can get this show on the road. I want to get home sometime tonight." Landry could tell that she meant business and knew there was no point in trying to stop her. They got out of the car and Landry pocketed the keys. They walked over to the wooden fence.

"Okay. I'll climb up and over the fence first. Then, you climb up and I'll help you over," Landry said, feeling awfully glad at that moment that she wore her boots.

She climbed up the fence and jumped over with no problem. Ms. Millie climbed it, too, without a problem and Landry was silently impressed by that. When Ms. Millie got to the top of the fence, she just threw her body towards Landry without even trying to land on the ground. Landry used all of her might to catch her but Ms. Millie fell right on top of her and they both went to the ground in a heap as Landry heard something that sounded like a rip. They got up and started to brush themselves off. Landry looked over at Ms. Millie.

"Where's your skirt?" she asked as she saw that Ms. Millie was standing there with her shirt and shoes on along with a half slip in place of the skirt."

Ms. Millie looked down in shock. They both looked at the fence and saw that Ms. Millie's skirt was hanging there torn in two where she had caught it on a nail. It was a pretty silk skirt that was now ruined.

"I told you that you should have stayed in the car." Landry scolded her. "That nice skirt is ruined because of your stubbornness."

"I didn't like that color, anyway," Ms. Millie said as she started walking the pasture in her half-slip.

Landry just shook her head and followed behind her. They were walking and talking about everything that had happened in town and Ms. Millie was still fussing about her bracelet being gone. Landry heard something behind them and turned around quickly to see if someone was following them. It was a dark night and she was thankful that the pasture had a couple of security lights to give at least a little light. She didn't see anybody and turned back around and started walking to catch up with Ms. Millie who was still talking.

They were making good progress when Landry heard the noise again. It sounded like a snort or growl to her. She stopped and turned back around to see the biggest bull she had ever seen. He was stomping his hooves and blowing out of his nose.

Landry turned back around and yelled, “Run, Ms. Millie!”

Ms. Millie looked back at Landry and said, “What are you talk–” She stopped talking when she saw the big bull. They both started running as fast as they could. Landry decided to run to the left away from Ms. Millie, hoping the bull would follow her since she could run faster with her boots. But, the bull was dead set on running for Ms. Millie.

Landry kept running as fast as she could so that she could at least get to the gate and climb over to unlock and open it before Ms. Millie got there. She got over the gate and was about to open it when she looked back. Ms. Millie was running faster than Landry would have ever imagined she could. The security light hit on her and Landry was immediately aware of why the bull was chasing her and not Landry.

“Ms. Millie, take your shirt off,” she yelled. “Your shirt is bright red. He’s aiming for it. Take it off and throw it behind you.”

Ms. Millie never broke stride. She grabbed the front of her shirt and ripped it open, buttons flying everywhere. She got it off and put it above her head. She threw it in the wind and kept running. The red shirt landed on the horns of the bull and he stopped to shake his head and get it off of him.

Ms. Millie was still running ninety to nothing and got to the gate just as Landry opened it for her. Landry closed and locked the gate back and heard a loud thud. She turned around and saw Ms. Millie laying on her back on the ground. Her eyes were closed and she was laying there in all her glory–camisole, half-slip, knee high hose and new suede shoes that were covered in bull poop. Lots of bull poop.

Landry walked over and saw that she was breathing. In fact, she was sucking in air so fast that it was a wonder she didn't hyperventilate. About that time, Landry noticed two headlights in the distance. Steve and Denise pulled up beside them in the Mule utility machine they used to drive around the farm in. Denise was getting out of the passenger side before Steve even stopped the vehicle. Steve jumped out next and ran up to see what was going on. He took one look at Ms. Millie on the ground in her underclothes and immediately turned his back to them.

"I'm sorry, Millie. I didn't realize you weren't dressed," he said.

Denise walked up and looked at them. "What is going on, Landry? Millie, are you alright?"

Landry told them what had happened. Ms. Millie had still not moved a muscle.

"We happened to be sitting on the porch and heard a ruckus. We jumped up and saw you two by the gate." Steve said, his back still turned.

In an almost whispered voice Ms. Millie said, "Denise, she's trying to kill me. Please help me. Call the law. I don't think I'll make it through any more of her shenanigans."

"Ms. Millie, I am not trying to kill you. Things just–

well, they just happen when we're together. Stop telling people that I'm trying to harm you. One day, somebody is going to think you're serious." Landry had her hands on her hips and was looking down at Ms. Millie.

Denise took all this in and then she took charge. "Okay, this is what we're going to do. We're going to put Millie in the back of the Mule and I'll drive her up to the house. I'll get her settled in a chair on the porch and come back down here to get you two. We'll drive back up to the house and Steve can get a can of gas from the shed and take Landry back to the car. I'll get Ms. Millie in the house–after I take off those poop covered shoes and throw them away–and get her cleaned up. I have some clothes she can put on."

Ms. Millie only heard one thing Denise said and she had misunderstood that. "I am not riding on the back of a mule to the house. I have already encountered a bull and I don't intend to deal with any other animals tonight."

The other three looked at each other in confusion for a minute. Then a light bulb went off in her head and Landry spoke up, "Ms. Millie, we aren't putting you on a mule. That's what this vehicle is called. It's a Mule utility vehicle. We're going to lay you down in the back of it so you won't get poop all over it."

"Oh, well I guess that's ok." Ms. Millie sat up on the ground and tried to get up. She was weak from running so hard, though, so Denise and Landry helped her up. Steve still wouldn't turn around for fear of seeing Ms. Millie in a state of undress. When they got her in the back, Denise drove her up to the house.

Landry looked around and saw Steve still standing with his back turned. His shoulders were shaking and Landry heard him laughing.

"I'm sorry, Landry. I didn't think I was going to e able to hold it in any longer. She was laying there sprawled out with just that camisole, half-slip, those knee high hose and those poop covered shoes. I've never in my life seen such a sight." He was laughing so hard he could hardly breathe.

Landry looked at him and she started laughing too. They stood there and just cackled every time they looked at one another.

Denise drove back up to get them and got out before they could get in. "Just a minute. I have to get my giggles out before I go back to Millie. Did y'all see her lying there? Every time I think about how she looked, I want to burst out laughing. Now that I know she's not hurt, I just have to get it out of me."

They all laughed until they had tears in their eyes. They finally stopped and got in the Mule to head back to the house. When they drove up, Ms. Millie was sitting in a rocking chair on the porch with a mad look on her face. Steve and Landry headed to the shed to get the gas can while Denise helped Ms. Millie in the house.

Chapter 8

On the way back to her car, Landry got serious again. She looked at Steve and said, "I'm positive that there was a full tank of gas in my car when I left to go pick up Ms. Millie. I filled it up yesterday morning to be sure I had a full tank. My car doesn't use a lot of gas. In fact, a full tank could probably get me to South Carolina and back here. It worries me that somebody might have sabotaged my car, Steve. They would have had to do it at the bus station since my car was in the garage at the apartment building and nobody can get in there without a key card. That would mean that somebody followed me to Wrigley Springs and messed with the car while I was preoccupied helping Ms. Millie get off the bus."

Steve shook his head. "That's disturbing, Landry. Is there anyone you suspect that could have done this?"

"No. But with the kidnappings and murder going on who knows what might happen? Until we know who's doing these horrible things, I don't know exactly who to trust." They pulled up to her car and got out. Steve checked everything out on the car and then put the gas in.

"Looks like nobody bothered it while it was here. You know, you might have a leak in the gas tank but I'd be surprised by that since I don't smell any gas fumes." Steve looked puzzled. "You go ahead and I'll follow you back to the farm."

Landry drove the car back and nothing seemed to be

wrong with it. She parked and got out and waited on Steve while he took the can back to the shed. They walked in the house and through the kitchen to the den where they heard the TV.

Landry entered the den and stopped in her tracks. Here sat the woman who just over an hour ago was laying in front of a pasture telling people to call the law because Landry was trying to kill her. Now, here she was looking like the queen of Sheba. She was reared back in a recliner with a white terry cloth robe on with white fuzzy slippers and a turban on her head. She was eating popcorn, drinking sweet tea and laughing hysterically at some sitcom on TV.

"What. Are. You. Doing?" Landry asked her.

Ms. Millie looked up and immediately stopped laughing. She put on a pitiful, sad look and said, "I'm trying to get my strength back up. Denise let me take a shower and she gave me some things to wear. I was thirsty from all that running, so she offered me some tea. I just hope that I don't wind up in the hospital from exposure or dehydration."

Landry rolled her eyes and said, "Well, we need to get going. I need to get you home to your own bed so that you can rest and we need to get out of Steve and Denise's hair." She turned around and told them, "Thank y'all so much for all that you did for us. We'll find a way to repay you one day."

Ms. Millie got up out of the recliner and told Denise that she would return her things to her after she washed them. Denise told her there was no hurry. Steve walked them outside and to the car. Ms. Millie had a hard time getting in with the turban on her head but refused to take it off. They told Steve goodbye and drove away.

"I can't believe that as soon as my feet hit the ground from the bus, you have been trying to hinder my getting back to my house, Landry." Ms. Millie sounded irritated.

"You sure looked like you were having the time of your life in front of that TV back there. I did not do any of this purposely. I asked you to stay in the car until I got Steve to get us some gas. If you had done what I asked, you would still have your nice clothes and new shoes that are now in the trash," Landry said defiantly.

"Hmph. I guess you could have buried me in that outfit when you came back to find me dead." Ms. Millie growled.

"I guess we're even now," Landry said. "You saved me from a bull when I was a child and now I saved you from one."

Ms. Millie just said, "Hmph."

They drove back to Bobwhite Mountain in silence. Landry stopped at the gas station and filled up before she took Ms. Millie home. When they got to the house, Landry took all of her luggage inside and made sure nobody had bothered anything in the house while she was in Mississippi. She then told Ms. Millie that none of them could be alone at the bookstore until these kidnappings and murder were solved. Of course, Ms. Millie talked all big and said that she could handle herself and that nobody would dare try to kidnap her.

"Ms. Millie, I'm tired and irritable. Don't push it with

me. None of us will be alone in the bookstore. None of us. I'll work the mornings with you until Maisy comes in after school. You and Maisy will leave at the same time when Maisy's mom comes to pick her up. I'll also ask Maisy to work on Saturdays with me until we find Jenna. Do you understand?" Landry asked her.

Ms. Millie looked shocked that Landry had stood up to her. She told her that she understood and now she had to go to bed.

Landry barely got out the door before Ms. Millie slammed it and locked it.

Magnolia Place was in her headlights. She felt like she'd been gone for days. She parked in the garage and walked into the lobby. Landry was startled to see so many people there at this time on a Saturday night. Then she noticed Wyatt and ran over to him.

"What's going on? Did you find Jenna?" Landry asked.

That's when she saw Mary Goode. She was crying uncontrollably.

"What is it Mary? Is everything alright?" She walked over to give her a hug.

Mary's voice was shaking and she said, "No, Landry. Nothing is alright. Penney went for her jog after she got off from the boutique. She never came home. She has been taken." Mary said the last sentence with a scream.

Landry looked at Wyatt. "Is this true? Penney's also missing?"

Wyatt nodded his head sadly. "From everything Mary

is telling me, yes. We can assume that she was taken by the same person who took Jenna."

Landry sent up a prayer for both girls as well as their parents. She asked the Lord to please keep them safe until they were found.

Wyatt asked Mary to go to the apartment and bring him a couple of photos of Penney. When she came back with them, he took her into the conference room behind Lisa's desk and questioned her. She asked that Landry come with her.

He asked Mary if there was anybody that Penney had mentioned that she had a problem with. Mary told him no, that Penney got along with everyone. He asked a few more questions and then told them that he'd be doing a press conference in the morning before church about Penney. They'd have the fliers and posters ready to be put up by then. He told Mary that they would do everything in their power to bring both girls back home safely.

When Mary went back upstairs to her apartment to wait on any news, Wyatt turned to Landry. "This is going to cause this town to go into a panic. Three women kidnapped. One of them found murdered. I've lived here my entire life and nothing like this has ever happened. We've scoured the area up at Sky High for any signs of a rope that might have been used to strangle Carla. We haven't found it yet. The autopsy isn't complete but Margie has told me that she was strangled and it looks like she was hit in the head with a blunt object like a rock."

It was then that Wyatt noticed Landry spinning her

ring around on her finger. She was also taking in some deep breaths through her nose. He sat there quietly while she tried to compose herself. He knew that both of the missing girls meant a lot to her and he was praying he would find them soon.

When Landry said that she was doing alright, they walked out of the conference room and ran into Adam.

"Adam. What are you doing here?" Landry asked, surprised to see him there.

"Wyatt texted me and said you might need me to be here with you for a while."

Wyatt spoke up. "It's not just Jenna now, Adam. Penney Goode is missing, too."

Adam looked shocked. "What?" he lowered his voice and said, "Oh no, Wyatt. We have someone going around our town kidnapping young girls. Not to mention that Carla is dead. Do you have any leads? What can we do to help you? This has got to stop." Adam turned to Landry and put his arm around her shoulders.

"I already told Landry that I do have some information about Carla's case that I want to run by the both of you. I asked if you two could come by my house tomorrow after church. I'll grill out for us and we can discuss things privately." Wyatt looked at his friend and Adam noticed he looked drawn and worried.

"Of course. We'll see you at church tomorrow and come out to your house from there," Adam replied.

"Sounds good. Now, please get Landry upstairs. From what she implied, she had a rough day even before all of this happened with Penney. See y'all tomorrow." Wyatt turned around and left to go back to the Sheriff's Department.

Chapter 9

After Adam walked her to her apartment door, Landry told him that she just wanted to get a hot shower and go to bed. He went in and got Zep to take him on a short walk. Landry got her nightclothes ready and got the coffee pot set for the morning. She made herself a ham sandwich and grabbed a diet soda out of the fridge. She finished eating just as Adam brought Zep back.

When Adam left, she loved on Zep for a few minutes and put fresh food and water down for him. She also gave him some more treats. Landry then got her shower and dressed for bed. She set the alarm to get her up the next morning and then laid there tossing and turning in bed as she couldn't stop thinking about everything that went on tonight. She knew with absolute certainty that she had a full tank of gas before she left for Wrigley Springs, so that puzzled her. Then she started thinking about Jenna and Penney. Landry couldn't get the image of Carla out of her head. She prayed and asked the Lord to protect the other two girls and keep them from ending up with the same fate. She finally drifted off to sleep.

After church the next day, she and Adam followed Wyatt to his house. This was the first time she had been to Wyatt's house and she found out that it was just outside of town in a subdivision. It was a quaint little home that had a white wooden fence around most of it. The house was painted a grayish blue color and had burgundy shutters. The front door was also painted burgundy. There was an oak tree in the backyard and its leaves had already turned a beautiful shade of orange for the fall. There was also a nice large deck back there.

They all pulled up in the driveway and Wyatt jumped out and opened the gate for them to all park in the side yard. When they entered the house, Landry noticed it was exceptionally neat and clean for a bachelor. She guessed that came from him being married for several years before his wife passed away. Judy Collins had died from an aneurysm that had burst. She and Wyatt had dated throughout high school and had married right after graduation.

Landry had made some ham roll ups that morning to bring for them to munch on before they grilled out. She had them in the cooler that she brought in from her car. She took them out and put them on the counter. Adam had brought sodas and chips with salsa, which he added to the counter.

Landry excused herself to the bathroom to change clothes. She had worn a dress to church that morning but had brought some jeans and a t-shirt with her so that she could get comfortable for the afternoon. When she got back to the den, Wyatt made them all something to drink and passed out paper plates. They made their snacks and took everything to the den where they sat down to talk.

"I have some things to tell you both about the investigation." Wyatt popped one of the ham roll ups in his mouth. "We've gotten quite a bit of information from our questioning of people that worked at the bank with Carla."

He wiped his hands and mouth off with a napkin and continued. "First of all, I found out that Carla used to date Dave Lemke, who dates Hannah Torres, Lisa's roommate, now. From everything I heard, their breakup wasn't pretty. Dave found out that Carla was cheating on him and they had it out. I'm going to question Dave about it tomorrow, but it seems to be common knowledge among the workers at the bank." Wyatt reached for his soda and drank about half of it in one chug.

Landry looked at him and said, "I'm surprised that Lisa didn't mention that when we were talking about Carla's murder. I guess it slipped her mind. Have you interviewed Hannah yet?"

"Not yet. She's on the list for tomorrow, too. I did interview most of the other workers at the bank, though. It seems that Carla got around." Wyatt sighed and put his head in his hands for a second. He straightened back up and told them, "She's been having an affair with Kevin Dent, who is the vice president of the bank. Mr. Dent's a married man. His wife is Ariel Dent and every single person I talked to told me that Ariel has a whopper of a temper. They say she's come into the bank on several occasions and had yelling sessions with her husband behind the closed doors of his office. I tried to interview both of the Dents but it seems they went out of town to Vegas this weekend. I've called them to meet me at my office tomorrow when they're back in town."

Adam looked up from his plate and added, "Man, that

sounds like a crime waiting to happen. Affair, jealous wife with a temper, prominent man with no desire to have the affair known." He shook his head.

"Yeah it sure does. Of course, they could have had nothing to do with Carla's murder but they're my prime suspects at the moment. I have a full day of interviews tomorrow with them as well as Dave Lemke and Hannah. I also have a sneaky feeling that there'll be more details coming to light before this is over. Of course, now that Jenna and Penney are missing, I wonder if all of this dirt even matters. There could be a dangerous kidnapper and killer on the loose that we don't even know." Wyatt looked stressed out and worried.

Landry spoke up with her own concerns. "I'm so worried about Jenna and Penney. They're so young and I know they have to be frightened and confused wherever they are. I refuse to believe that they'll suffer the same consequences as Carla. We have to find them."

She kicked off her shoes and put her legs under her on the couch. She proceeded to tell them both about what happened to her and Ms. Millie the night before. When she was done with her story, Adam and Wyatt both burst out laughing. They laughed and laughed and then Wyatt said, "I can just see Ms. Millie running from that bull. That's probably the only thing she has ever backed down from in her life."

Adam pointed at him. "And, she lost most of her clothes in the process. She is so hoity toity all the time. I know that had to embarrass her." They both started laughing again.

Landry looked at them, "You're both acting like schoolboys. Poor Ms. Millie. She was dog tired from outrunning that bull."

"You mean to tell me that you didn't laugh? I know you did because there's absolutely no way you couldn't have." Wyatt laughed.

"So hard that I cried. Steve and I had a hard time holding it together until Denise took Ms. Millie up to the house. We cracked up as soon as they were out of earshot." Landry grinned.

The guys laughed and Landry said, "There's a serious note to all of that. I purposely filled up my car the day before I went to pick Ms. Millie up in Wrigley Springs. After filling it up, I went straight to Magnolia Place and left it in the garage. Nobody except the people who live or work there have access to the parking garage. I also checked the security camera footage from that night and nobody was in the garage at all overnight. The reason we had to get help from Steve and Denise that night is that my car ran out of gas on that dark road. I can't figure it out. I didn't stop anywhere on the way to the bus station and when we left the bus station, we got right on the road home and didn't stop anywhere. It's a complete puzzle to me."

She looked at both of the guys and they looked confused as well. "That's strange," Wyatt said. "Are you sure you didn't stop anywhere on the way there after you left your garage?"

"I'm positive. That's the whole reason for my getting

gas the day before. I didn't want to have to stop on the way to Wrigley Springs." She was adamant about it.

"That worries me," Adam replied. "Maybe there's a leak in the gas tank or something. I'll take it to Corey Brand's tomorrow when I have a break." He referred to the mechanic in town. "He can check it out."

"Thanks. That'd be great. I drove it to church this morning and then out here without a problem," Landry told him.

They all stood up and Wyatt went outside to start the grill while Adam and Landry put the steaks on a plate. They walked out of the back door and onto the deck.

"Hey, Wyatt," Landry said, "do you have any kind of music around here?"

Wyatt laughed and went back inside. He came out with an old boom box that had a radio. Adam looked at it like it was something from outer space. "What's that? I can't believe you still have that thing."

"It still works. No reason to upgrade if it's perfectly fine." Landry grinned. She loved it. Wyatt plugged it in and she found an 80's channel on the radio. She was in heaven. They cranked it up and Wyatt put the steaks on the grill along with some corn on the cob and potatoes that he had prepped last night and put in the fridge.

Adam and Landry started dancing to the music and Wyatt was laughing at them. He hadn't felt this happy in a long time. He still missed Judy and all of their craziness. It was so good to have his friends around him. He walked over to an outdoor building and pulled out some cornhole boards and bean bags. They took turns playing with each other and watching the food on the grill.

When the food was done, they went back inside to eat. After they were done, they all sat back. “I need a nap now,” Adam said. “That was some wonderful food, Wyatt. You haven’t lost your touch.”

“Thanks, man. It’s good to have people to cook for. I love to grill out,” Wyatt replied.

Landry and Adam got up and cleaned up the mess. They loaded the dishwasher and wiped down the counters.

“Well, guys, this has been fun but I have to be going. I have laundry to do and I need to check on Zep,” Landry told them.

“I’ll follow you and stop by and take him for a walk. Then I’m heading to Mom’s to make sure she’s doing alright,” Adam said.

They got their things together and told Wyatt goodbye before they left for home. Adam followed Landry home and took Zep out. He dropped him back at the apartment and he and Landry said their goodbyes before he headed to the B&B to check on his Mom.

Landry gathered up all of the dirty laundry and put a load in the washer. She fed Zep and then decided to call Lisa. She had a few questions for her now that she knew that Dave Lemke had previously dated Carla.

“Hello?” Lisa answered on the first ring.

“Hi, Lisa. I hope you aren’t in the middle of something important. If you are, I can just talk to you tomorrow,” Landry said.

"Absolutely not. In fact, I'm bored out of my mind. There was an emergency at the vet's office and Jarred is the one on call this weekend, so he had to report to duty." Lisa laughed. "We were supposed to go hiking today and I got all my household chores done yesterday."

"Why don't you come over? I know this building is technically your work, but come to my apartment. I'm doing laundry and really want to stay inside for the rest of the day since Zep is by himself so much. I also need to make the snack for the kids tomorrow at Jasmine Bloom. Tomorrow is a movie and snack day in the Children's Room," Landry told her. "Tomorrow's movie is Charlotte's Web. Say, do you happen to have any pretzel sticks?"

"I do. I have a whole bag that I bought last week. Do you need me to bring them to you?" Lisa asked.

"Please. I have all of the other things I need and there's no baking involved. You can help me assemble them while we talk. Lisa, please don't stop anywhere on the way here. Just come straight to the parking garage. I'm being overly cautious but, until the murderer and kidnapper is caught, I just want us all to stay safe."

Lisa assured her she would be very careful and would be there soon.

Landry went and swapped out the clothes to the dryer and put in another load of bedclothes. She then went into the kitchen and started a pot of coffee.

She was sitting on the couch playing with Zep when Lisa knocked on the front door. Landry let her in and Lisa picked up Zep and snuggled him. Zep was in heaven. He loved Lisa.

"Here are the pretzels." Lisa handed her the bag and went to wash her hands. They went into the kitchen and Landry took out a pack of chocolate cookies with double the white icing in the middle, a small tube of white icing and a bag of chocolate chips. She placed the bag of pretzels on the table with the other things.

She made them both a mug of coffee and they sat down at the table. "Lisa," Landry started, "I didn't know that Dave Lemke used to date Carla. I just found that out today."

"Yep. They had a bad breakup, too. She was cheating on him and he found out. Hannah said that Dave's still hurt by that," Lisa told her. "But, Landry, there's just no way that he would have killed Carla if that's where your train of thought is going. He's such a sweet guy, and I just can't see him doing that, especially since he's with Hannah now and has moved on."

Landry took the cookies out of the bag and started to assemble the first one so that Lisa could see how it was done. She took eight of the pretzel sticks and stuck four on each side of the cookie. Then, she used the white icing and put two small dots on the lower part of the cookie. She put a chocolate chip on top of each dot and showed it to Lisa.

"It's a spider? That's so cute! That's perfect for the movie tomorrow. The kids will love it!" Lisa was impressed.

"I think so, and, according to the files we keep, none of the kids are allergic to any of these ingredients." Landry picked up another cookie and handed it to Lisa. "Let's make some more spiders."

Lisa laughed and started assembling her spider. "Back to what we were saying. I know Wyatt's going to talk to Dave. Hannah's worried about it, too."

"Why's she worried? Doesn't he have an alibi for the timeframe of Carla's murder?" she asked as she put the white icing on another cookie.

"I'm not sure. I do know that he and Hannah were going to go out to eat and to a movie the night you found Carla. Hannah said that Dave called and told her that he was sick. He said he thought it was food poisoning and that he couldn't go anywhere. He lives alone in his apartment and later he told Hannah that he took some nausea medicine and finally dropped off to sleep. Not much of an alibi, since nobody actually saw him," Lisa told her and put a completed cookie on the plate Landry had on the table.

Landry sighed and shook her head. "I hope Wyatt can find the person who did this to Carla and also kidnapped Jenna and Penney before anyone else is taken. I also pray that the girls are alright and will be back home soon."

They sat in silence for a few minutes, assembling the cookies until they were done. "That should be enough. We don't have many kids on Mondays. Everly Watson from the 3rd floor brings her twins, Bridget and Ridge. I know she has to love the time alone, even if it's just for a couple of hours. With Logan doing his residency at the hospital, he's there all day and into the night. When he is at home, he's pouring over medical books and patient charts. She seems happy enough, though," Landry told her. "We have a few other local moms that also take advantage of the time off. I think we have six children that come on Mondays right now."

Landry went over to the coffeepot and refilled their mugs. They walked out on the balcony and Zep followed them outside.

"I've been meaning to tell you that we have an event scheduled this month for the event room upstairs. It's a retired cops reunion. Every year, they take turns and have it in their hometowns. This is Josh's year, so he's having it in the event room," Lisa explained.

"Oh, Lisa. I hope you gave Josh a discount on the room. I hate for him to have to pay a lot since he works here." Landry bent down and petted Zep. She pulled her legs up into the chair and took a sip of her coffee.

"I did. Miss Tildie always told me to make sure that if any employee wanted to use the room, to give them a good discount. I did that for Josh since he's a lobby assistant." Lisa nodded her head.

Landry told her thank you.

"We also had someone schedule one for October and well, you aren't going to like this one. I almost turned them down but I know how hard you're working this first year to show a profit, so I agreed." Lisa looked at her hesitantly.

"Uh-oh. Go ahead. Tell me." Landry braced herself.

Lisa looked down at the ground and was fidgeting. "It's a realtor convention."

Landry looked at her in surprise. "That doesn't sound

bad. Are they known to be rough in the event room or someth–' Landry paused her mug halfway to her mouth. "Oh no. Pam. Pam Rivers will be in my building in my event room for the night. Ugh."

"Yep. Like I said, it was on the tip of my tongue to tell her to go elsewhere and that she was not welcome here, but with the profit clause in the will, I thought better of it," Lisa said quietly.

Landry looked at Lisa and saw that her friend was worried about accepting Pam's group. "You did the right thing, Lisa. We can't refuse people the use of the event room just because we don't like them personally. I mean, Pam has never done anything to me. The problem I have with her is the way she treated, and still treats, Adam. It'll be fine."

"Thank you, Landry. I hope it will. I know Pam is a snake in the grass, but I'm just hoping that she'll behave herself while her colleagues are around her. Now, I have to get going. I want to get home before dark. Hannah went to visit her grandma at the nursing home, but she should be home when I get there. We're in the habit now of being in before dark unless we are with someone else. We lock up the house like Fort Knox before we go to bed." Lisa stood up.

"That's fine, Lisa. Thank you for coming and helping me with the snack. Thanks for the pretzel sticks, too. I'm going to walk out with you since I want to run down to the third floor to check on Mary Goode. I get sick to my stomach when I think about Penney and Jenna being missing. I know Mary's beside herself." She walked Lisa out. They both got on the elevator and Landry told Lisa goodbye and got off on Mary's floor. Lisa continued to the lobby to go home.

Chapter 10

Mary threw open the front door as soon as Landry knocked on it. She asked, "Did they find her? Is Penney coming home?"

Landry looked at her sympathetically. "I'm sorry, Mary. I haven't heard any more news. I wanted to stop by and check on you and see if you need anything. I know all you truly need is Penney to be found, but maybe there's something I can do for you in the meantime."

"Please come in," she said and Landry walked into the living room and sat down. "I feel so lost and useless. I'm her Momma. I'm supposed to keep her safe. I just want my baby home."

Landry looked at Mary and saw that she was drawn and frail. She had dark circles under her eyes and her hair was tangled. Landry knew Mary had probably not slept a wink since Penney had gone missing.

"Let me make you some tea and maybe a sandwich, Mary. You need to keep your strength up so that Penney won't be so worried about you when she gets back. I'd be more than happy to sit here if you want to go get a shower and maybe a short nap. I'll be right here beside the phone in case there's any news." Landry tried to think of anything to do that would make Mary at least get a nap.

Mary looked hesitant but finally said, "That'd be so kind of you. Do you promise to come get me if there's any news of any kind?"

Landry silently sighed with relief. "Of course I do. Would you like me to make your tea and a sandwich first?"

"No. I would like some tea, but I can't eat anything right now. I think I'll go get a quick shower and then come drink the tea. I'll try to lie down for a few minutes if you promise me that you'll be here the entire time." Mary was crying and wiping her eyes with her handkerchief.

"I promise," Landry assured her.

Mary got up and went to take a shower. When she was done, Landry made her tea and put a half of a ham sandwich beside it on a plate, hoping that she would take just a couple of bites. They talked about Penney and Jenna and Mary told her that she felt in her heart that the girls were still alright. Landry told her that she did, too. Eventually, Mary took a few bites of the sandwich and then got up to take a nap.

Landry cleaned up the kitchen, since she knew Mary hadn't done anything since she found out Penney was missing. She then tidied up the living room and sat down. She turned the TV on very low volume and watched some game shows while she tried to think of where those girls could be.

Mary slept for three hours and then arose. After the sleep, the shower and the little bit of sandwich, she looked somewhat better than Landry had found her. Mary thanked her so much for coming over and trying to make her feel a little better.

"Listen, Mary. If you ever want to come to my apartment and visit me and Zep, just show up. I can make you something to eat and we can talk. If you don't want to leave your apartment, I'll be glad to come here and do exactly what I did today. You have to eat and rest some, Mary. You can't let yourself get sick. You have to stay strong for Penney." Landry went over and hugged her.

"I'll remember that. I go every day down to James Larson's apartment for a bit to make sure he's alright. I don't stay as long as I usually do because I have to get back here in case there's news. He's doing really well now and I don't think he'll need me to help him much longer. I called Brad, his son, and told him what had happened and he understood. I've canceled all of my other clients for now. I know I can't be away for long because I need the money to pay my bills, but I'm hoping that Penney is back home soon." Mary looked helpless and it hurt Landry to her soul.

"There's one thing I can do for you, Mary. Don't worry about your rent while Penney's gone and you are out of work. I'll instruct Lisa to mark it as paid. That's not much, but it'll help out some," Landry said to her as she hugged her again and told her goodbye.

Mary started crying again and said through her tears, "That's the kindest thing anyone has ever done for me. You have no idea how much that means, Landry."

Landry smiled and went back to her apartment. Zep met her at the front door and started yipping. She knew that yip. He wanted treats. She put him some down and got her clothes out to fold. She finished them and got ready for bed. It had been a long, tiring day.

Before she went to sleep, she called Ms. Millie and

told her to come straight to Magnolia Place in the morning. She told her to park in the extra parking slot next to her Bug and that she'd meet her in the lobby so that they could walk over to Jasmine Bloom together. She didn't want anybody parking in the back parking lot at the bookstore for the time being.

The next morning, she got the spider treats and met Ms. Millie downstairs. They walked across the street and opened up the bookstore. Landry put the kid's treats in the Children's Room and straightened up. She got the movie ready to play and then went to the back office to start the coffeepot. Ms. Millie got the cash register going for the day and dusted the counters. They turned the sign on the door to open and began their day.

Before customers started coming in, Ms. Millie looked at Landry and said, "I still can't believe my grandson lifted my bracelet. The more I think about it, the more I know that I have to tell Vanessa about it. They need to rein that child in before he becomes a lifetime criminal."

"Ms. Millie, you don't even know if it was Wesley who took it or not. You don't even know if anybody took it. You might've just lost it." Landry gave Ms. Millie a stern look. "It could do real damage to the relationship between you and Vanessa if you accuse him falsely. You need to wait and be sure that nobody finds it before you tell her anything except that you lost it and for her to be on the lookout for it."

Ms. Millie got a belligerent look on her face and started to say something back when a customer walked in.

She turned to greet them with a smile and Landry escaped into the back office.

Later that morning, the kids arrived and Landry sat in the Children's Room with them while they watched Charlotte's Web. The spider cookies were a huge hit and they all loved pulling off the 'legs' to eat them first. After the kids had left, Landry cleaned up the room and closed the door. She turned around and saw Adam at the counter. "What're you doing here?" she asked him.

Ms. Millie held up a styrofoam plate and said, "This angel brought us lunch. I'm going to the office to eat mine. I put the sign on the door that we are closed for lunch. You two can eat in the Children's Room." She cackled as she staked her claim to the desk in the office.

Landry she walked up to greet Adam, she noticed his smile and that cute dimple of his. She caught her breath as she realized that her stomach had butterflies in it. She was happy to see him there. "What's going on here?" she thought to herself. "Maybe I do have feelings for him."

Adam said, "Earth to Landry. What are you daydreaming about?" That got her attention.

"Nothing. Just thinking. What did you bring us for lunch?" She tried to act normal but what she just felt was throwing her equilibrium off.

"I stopped at the diner and got the special for the day. Homemade chicken pot pie, a salad and hash brown casserole. I also got us each a slice of pie. The pie today is blueberry. Hope you and Ms. Millie like it," he smiled.

"It smells wonderful and I'm starving. Come on, let's

go sit at the tiny picnic tables in the Children's Room." She laughed and opened the door.

They sat down and were eating the food, which Landry declared delicious. All of a sudden, they heard a loud banging on the front door. Adam jumped up to get it and ran right into Ms. Millie coming from the back office.

"Who's doing all that banging? Can't they read? Why did I even put the sign up if nobody pays attention to it." She looked fit to be tied. "How dare somebody interrupt lunch time?"

Adam just stared at her with a face that said 'are you serious right now' and walked up to the door. It was Wyatt. Adam opened the door and let him in and then locked it back.

"I should've known it was you. You never did follow rules. How you became a lawman, I'll never understand. Now, I'm going back to eating before my food gets cold." Ms. Millie looked disgusted with Wyatt.

He just looked at Adam and Landry with a question on his face. They both shrugged and told him to come to the Children's Room. When he walked in, he laughed and told them that they looked like those clowns in the little cars at the circus sitting at that tiny table. He decided to sit on the floor. He propped his arms up on his knees. Landry thought he looked tired.

"So, what have you two been up to so far today?" he asked them.

"I had a female client come in today to change her will. She comes in at least every three months to change it, depending on which of her four children she's angry with." Adam shook his head. "She's going to spend all of the money she has changing that will before she passes away."

Wyatt and Landry laughed and Landry said, "Well, I watched Charlotte's Web and ate a spider cookie with the kids. I just can't get Carla and the two girls out of my head. Any updates, Wyatt?"

"I've been doing interviews all morning. Margie called from the coroner's office this morning and let me know that, as best she can tell, Carla had been dead for a couple of days when we found her. That piece of information makes my investigation a lot harder. I've pretty much ruled Dave Lemke out since two days before we found Carla he worked at his dad's hardware store all day and went straight to pick up Hannah when he got off. Multiple people have told me that he was there all day at the hardware store and Hannah actually kept their movie tickets from that night to put in some kind of 'memory box' she has. We checked the video footage of the theater and they were there for the entire time. He and Hannah went back to her and Lisa's house and he fell asleep on the couch. Lisa said that when she got up at five the next morning, he was still there. He worked all of the next day at the store and then went over to his uncle's house to play poker and was there most of the night. Dave thinks that's where he got the food poisoning from." Wyatt explained.

Adam shook his head. "Did they find any kind of DNA on Carla that would be helpful?"

"No. She was laying in the muck and water in that well

too long for that. Margie did tell me something interesting, though. She says it looks like Carla was hit in the head with the butt of a pistol and knocked out before she was strangled. I guess whoever killed her and put her in the well didn't want anybody hearing a gunshot and come to investigate." Wyatt looked off into space like he was picturing the scenario. "We did take DNA samples from everyone at the bank. Probably won't do much good. I wish we could find the rope that killed Carla."

Landry asked him, "What about the Dent's? The bank president and his wife? Did you interview them yet?"

"I did. They came by the department early this morning. They were interviewed separately and Kevin admitted he was having an affair with Carla but swears he didn't kill her. He said he didn't know where she was going over the weekend but it wasn't with him. As you know, he and his wife, Ariel, went to Vegas this past weekend. He had a dinner meeting two nights before Carla was found and he left the bank the next night and went straight to the airport to meet Ariel so they could board the plane."

Adam looked at him and said, "You know, there's no way you can account for every minute of the 48 hours before we found Carla. Somebody could've had time to kill her between any of the times they said they had alibis."

Wyatt stood up and walked over to the little window in the Children's Room and looked out. "Yep. I think somebody's going to have to slip up for us to catch them. Ariel was very blunt in her interview. She told me that she knew Kevin was having an affair with Carla. She also said she didn't care. She told me as long as he put his paycheck in their bank account, she didn't care what he was doing with whom. I got the feeling she's probably seeing somebody else, too. How can anybody do that? I mean, if you want to act like that, why even get married? I'll never understand it." He sounded angry and sad. Landry knew he was thinking that he would have been faithful to Judy until he died and here these people were treating marriage like it was a game. She felt so bad for him.

Wyatt shook his head like he was trying to clear it. "Anyway, those are the interviews I did today. My deputies interviewed everybody at the bank. Not much came out of that."

Adam said, "I know this is a change of the subject, but is the town still planning on having the Fall Festival this weekend at the fairgrounds? I mean, with Carla being killed and Jenna and Penney still missing, is it going to happen as planned?"

Wyatt let out a big sigh. "Yep. The Mayor is bound and determined for it to happen. He said it's one of the biggest fundraisers for the volunteer fire department and that I'll just have to be sure everyone stays safe. I'll have all of my deputies there except for Cora. She'll stay behind and run the desk at the department. Chief Edmunds over in Wrigley Springs has said that he'll send all of his available police officers to help out. We'll make continuous announcements over the loudspeaker to remind everyone to not stray away from the festival by themselves and to stay in groups."

Adam got up and put his and Landry's trash in the can. "Well, you know I'll help to keep a watch on folks, too. I know this has to be so stressful for you, Wyatt."

Wyatt walked to the door. "Thanks, Adam. I need to run. I still have a lot to do today and I just want to find those girls and get them back home."

After he left, Landry looked at Adam and asked, "Do they have the Fall Festival every year? Is it a big deal?"

"Oh, yeah. There's rides, games, a hayride, lots of food vendors and all kinds of things. Like Wyatt said, all the money that's made goes to the volunteer fire department. It's a huge deal for Bobwhite Mountain. Even the celebrities that have houses on the mountain have been known to come. It really is fun. I just don't know how much fun it'll be this year with all that's going on."

Landry started towards the door to go back up front and Adam stopped her. He looked at her and said, "I know I promised Wyatt that I would keep an eye out at the festival, but I can do that while still walking around and taking everything in. Landry, would you be my date for the festival?"

Landry's mouth went dry and it took her a minute to speak. When she did, she said, "I'd love to be your date, Adam. Thank you so much for asking me."

Adam grinned. "I know we spend a lot of time together, but I guess this is our first official date."

He drew in a deep breath and said, "What I really want to ask you is if you and I–I mean–do you think we can date exclusively?"

“You mean I’ll have to tell all of the other guys that I’m dating that I can’t see them anymore?” She looked at him with her eyes wide.

He had a worried look on his face along with a frown. “Wha–”

Landry laughed and said, “I’m kidding you, Adam. I thought you would never ask me. Of course we can. There isn’t anyone else I want to spend time with.”

He let out a big breath that he’d been holding in and hugged her. He left the bookstore whistling and smiling. Ms. Millie was at the front counter and looked at him with a funny look on her face as he walked out the door.

“What’s got into him? Why does he seem so chipper?”

Landry smiled as she walked to the window and watched Adam walk down the street. “Well, Ms. Millie. Adam asked me to be his girl and I said yes.”

Ms. Millie’s eyes got big and she just shook her head and mumbled something that sounded to Landry like, “Oh, no. That boy’s been bitten by the love bug.”

Chapter 11

The rest of the week passed by without any leads on Jenna and Penney. Landry feared the worst but would not speak it out loud. She prayed every night for the girls to be alright and for them to come home soon.

Friday morning, she walked down to the lobby to meet Ms. Millie so they could walk to the bookstore. She saw Lisa sitting at her desk frowning while she was looking at some papers. Landry spoke to Garrett and walked over to Lisa's desk.

"What are you pondering, Lisa? You look deep in thought."

Lisa looked up and said, "Look at this. I was just looking at these fliers that were made up for the girls. I never realized how similar they look. Not so much in looks but they are about the same height, both are very slim and both have long blonde hair. See?" She pointed at the fliers.

Landry took the fliers in her hands to get a better look. "You're right. I never really paid any attention to that." She thought for a minute and said, "You know, Carla had short brown hair, was curvy and not very tall. Nothing at all like the girls. I've heard that usually if a person kidnaps several women, they usually have a 'type'. Like the victims remind the kidnapper of someone they knew or someone that made them mad. It's strange that these two look so much alike and Carla looked nothing like them."

Lisa nodded her head and Ms. Millie walked in from

the garage. "Let's go, Landry. No time to waste. We have to open the doors if we want to sell some books today."

Landry looked at Lisa and smiled as she shook her head in Ms Millie's direction. "I'm coming, Ms. Millie. Just give me a minute. I need to talk to Lisa about something."

She pulled Lisa to the back of the office and told her about Adam asking her to be his date. Lisa grinned and said, "It's about time. My cousin has been keen on you since the day you arrived in Bobwhite Mountain. This is great. I'm so happy for you both."

Landry could feel her face getting hot. "Lisa, we're just dating, not getting married. I just thought you should know since we'll be together at the festival tomorrow. You and Jarred are coming, aren't you?"

"Oh, yeah. We'll be there. Jarred is in charge of the cow this year, since he is a vet tech and all," Lisa said casually.

Landry got a very confused look on her face and was about to ask Lisa what she was talking about when she heard a booming voice behind her.

"Girl, are you coming? I'm going to walk on over. If you want to come with me, fine. I'm not going to be late opening up so that you can stand there and gossip with Lisa," Ms. Millie yelled.

"Coming," Landry told her and they went over to the bookstore.

That afternoon, Adam came into the bookstore. He walked to the back office where Landry was working on the computer and bent down and whispered in her ear. “You haven’t changed your mind about tomorrow, have you?”

A huge grin appeared on her face on her face, but didn’t look up. “You know, I have a boyfriend now and he’ll be angry if he sees you whispering in my ear.”

Adam jerked up and said, “Excuse me?”

She laughed and got up out of her chair. “Oh, it’s you. I thought it was somebody else.”

He laughed and put his hand over his heart and bent his knees. “Don’t do that to me, Landry. Do you have any idea how scared I was when I asked you to date me and only me? I couldn’t wipe the grin off my face all day after you agreed. I keep thinking I dreamed it. You made me very happy when you said yes.”

She looked into those crystal clear blue eyes and saw those dimples pop out on his face and she knew she was a goner. If he had asked her to fly to the moon with him at that moment, she would have beaten him to the spaceship.

Maisy walked in the front door at that moment and Landry shut down her computer. “I’m free now, Adam. So I’m going to take Zep for a walk. Want to come with us?”

“You bet. I have the afternoon off and I haven’t eaten today. What about you? Want to grab a bite to eat after we walk the little fuzzball?”

“Sounds good. I ate some yogurt and an apple for lunch. I’m really hungry.” They walked up front and told Ms. Millie and Maisy goodbye and went to get Zep.

After Zep’s long walk, Landry fed him and she and

Adam left to get something to eat. "Where do you want to go?" Adam asked her as they reached the lobby.

"I know this sounds strange but could we go to the Sky High? I would love a steak. Yours looked so good the last time we were there." She smiled at him.

"Landry, I know what you want and it's not a steak. You want to go back to the crime scene at the well. Wyatt really won't like that, you know," Adam said as they made their way out to the street and his car.

Landry knew she was treading on thin ice but she did want to go back to the well and look around.

"Come on, Adam. I just want to see if we might find some clues at the crime scene while there's still daylight. Wyatt and his deputies have combed over the place for a few days now. I'm sure we won't find anything but sometimes fresh eyes will pick up on something. I have to do something to try and get Jenna and Penney back. If their disappearances are related to Carla's, maybe there will be some little clue that was left behind," Landry begged.

How could he resist her? He couldn't. "Fine. But just know that I am throwing you under the bus if Wyatt catches us," he laughed.

As they rode up the chairlift to the Sky High Tavern, Landry looked over at the mountain on the other side. "Is that the mountain that the hikers like to climb?"

Adam looked over to where she was pointing. "Yep. A lot of the local hikers have been complaining because of the houses being built on the other side of that mountain. They're worried that eventually the residential area will get too close to this side where they love to hike. I personally agree with them. There are so many other places for homes. I don't like it when any landmarks native to this area are taken over by homes or businesses."

They reached the top of the mountain and jumped out of the chairlift. Since it was still light but would be getting dark soon, they decided to go to the well first. They walked past a couple of customers at the front door of the Sky High and continued on down the dirt road. They stopped along the way when Landry asked Adam about some of the plants and flowers that were growing there.

When they finally reached the area of the well, they split up and walked around in the woods closest to the well site. At one point, Adam thought he had found something. It looked like a large rock with blood on it but, after he examined it closer, he could tell that it was just a couple of the red leaves from the trees that had fallen on the rock and had been soaked with rain.

He was standing back up when he heard Landry yell. He went running in the direction of her scream and when he saw her, he yelled, "Landry, what is it? Are you alright?"

"Yeah. A limb fell out of a tree and onto the ground. I thought it was a snake." She looked at him sheepishly. "Sorry."

She started walking towards him and all of a sudden, face planted into the leaves and sticks on the ground in front of her. He started running to her again and said, "What in the world? What happened?"

She grimaced as she told him, “I tripped over a vine. I am so clumsy.”

“Are you alright?”

“I am but I fell on something hard and it is poking me in the stomach. I guess it’s a rock.” She got up on her knees and started pushing the leaves around to see what she had fallen on.

When she saw it, she looked up. “Adam, I know cell phones don’t work here since we discovered that the last time we were here. You need to go back to the Sky High and call Wyatt right away. Tell him to get here as soon as he can and to bring an evidence bag.” She stood up and backed away from what she had found.

Adam looked alarmed and went to her. “What is it, Landry? What did you find?”

She looked up into his eyes and said calmly. “I think I just found the rope that was used to kill Carla.”

She waited there for Adam to get back after calling Wyatt. She didn’t want to forget exactly where she was when she fell. Wyatt showed up in record time and she was glad since it was beginning to get dark. She showed him where the rope was and he used gloves to pick it up and bag it.

She explained to him, “When I fell, I felt something like a rock underneath me. When I brushed away the leaves, I saw the knot at the end of the rope. That’s what was poking into my stomach. Do you think there’ll be DNA on it, Wyatt?”

Wyatt looked at the evidence bag in his hand and

shook his head. “Hard to say. There’s a slight chance that there might be since it’s been covered up with leaves. I’ll get it to the lab right away. I can’t believe you found this. I had my deputies up here for days searching around. Why were the two of you up here, anyway?”

Adam dropped his head and looked at the ground. Landry said, “I’m starving, Adam. We better get to the Sky High and get some grub.” She started to walk away.

Wyatt grabbed her arm. “Good try, Landry. Answer my question.”

“It’s my fault. I begged Adam to bring me back here to look around while it was daylight. Sorry, Wyatt, but at least it paid off. I found something that could break this case for you.”

Wyatt shook his head and closed his eyes for a minute. “You have got to learn to let me do the investigating. Don’t get me wrong, I’m very appreciative that you found this rope, but the two of you can’t keep going off on your own to crime scenes. Adam, you know better.”

They all walked out of the woods and Wyatt asked them if they were going to stay and eat or if they wanted a ride back down to Adam’s car.

Landry looked at Adam and said, “If it’s all the same to you, I have the stuff to make spaghetti at home. Why don’t we just go back and eat at the apartment?”

Adam said that sounded great to him and Landry asked Wyatt if he wanted to come over and eat with them. He jumped at the chance and took them to Adam’s car. He told them that he was going to take the rope back to the department and would be by after that.

When they got back to Landry's, she made them both some iced tea and changed into some sweats. Adam played with Zep while she started making dinner. She told him that she was going to make what she called "Lunch Lady Spaghetti", since it was quick and didn't require her to boil the noodles. She told him that Ms. Millie had told her about it when she first got to Bobwhite Mountain and, since Ms. Millie had worked in the school lunchroom for 40 years, that's why she called it that.

She got everything in the casserole dish and put it in the oven. She had some frozen garlic bread and put that in there, too. She was just joining Adam and Zep when Wyatt showed up. He went and washed up and came back to the den where the others were watching TV and playing with Zep.

He walked over to the recliner that Landry had in the den and sat down and sighed heavily. "One of my deputies is on the way to the state crime lab with the rope you found." He looked at Landry. "I talked to them and because we still have two girls missing, in addition to Carla being dead, they're doing a rush job on the DNA for us. It'll still take longer than I want it to. I sure hope they can find something."

"So do I. I think about Jenna and Penney every minute of the day. I pray that they're both still alive and will come home soon." Landry got up and went into the kitchen.

She took the garlic bread out of the oven and checked on the spaghetti. It would be ready in just a few minutes.

She set the table and poured them all some sweet tea before she returned to the den.

Wyatt had his eyes closed but started talking again. "I've talked to the people that Carla worked with more than once and I've talked to her parents, friends and even some customers that go to the bank on a regular basis. Nobody can think of who might have kidnapped and killed her. Also, not one person knows who she was going to see that Friday after she got off of work. She just told everybody that she had out-of-town plans that weekend. The only possible lead in that direction is that her mom told me that Carla sometimes went up to their cabin in Pigeon Forge to be by herself and think about things. They said she had a key to the place and went many times. She would call them after she got there to let them know where she was. At this point, I'm assuming that was her plan before she was kidnapped." He opened his eyes. He looked so tired and frustrated.

Landry got up and told the guys to come eat. They all went to the kitchen and she got the spaghetti out of the oven. She gave Zep a few treats and then put the casserole dish in the middle of the table. Adam said the blessing and they all served themselves.

"This sure smells great, Landry," Wyatt told her as he dished up some in his plate. I love that it has lots of cheese, too."

"The smell alone would make you want to eat it even if you weren't hungry, which I am," Adam said.

Landry smiled as she got her own helping of food.

"That's the fresh garlic you guys smell. I love it, too."

They ate and the guys got seconds. They both said it was the best spaghetti they had ever had. Landry was happy that they enjoyed it so much. When they were done, the guys put the dishes in the dishwasher and they all went into the living room.

Wyatt stretched his back out and said, "I sure hate to eat and run, but I have to get back to the department. I have paperwork to do, and I really would love to get home at a decent time tonight and try to get some sleep." He turned to Landry and said, "Thank you for the meal. I really appreciate it. I kinda feel like a third wheel now that the two of you are a couple."

"That's nonsense and you know it," Adam laughed. "We're all friends and that will never change. You know you will always be welcomed by both of us."

Adam turned to Landry and explained, "I told Wyatt about us deciding to be exclusive. I hope you don't mind, but he's my best friend and I was so happy I had to tell someone." Landry laughed and said, "Of course I don't mind."

Wyatt slapped Adam on the back and said, "Thanks for that. Now, I'm going so you two can at least have a little time alone. I'll talk to you both sometime tomorrow."

After he left, they went back to the den where Zep was snoring on the couch pillow. He loved it in this room for some reason. Landry asked Adam how his mom was doing.

"Oh, she's much better. She's walking around and cooking for the guests at the B&B again. I've enjoyed spending more time with her, but I have some things I have to catch up on at work. Lots of paperwork and research that I put off last week." He smiled.

"Well, I'm glad you were there to help her out." Landry yawned right at that moment and Adam smiled.

"I'm going to get out of here, too. It's been a long day and we both need some rest." He got up and Landry walked him to the front door, while Zep didn't even look up.

As he was leaving, Adam hugged her and gave her a light kiss on her lips. "I hope you sleep well tonight, Landry. I'll be by the bookstore sometime tomorrow."

She thanked him and told him to be careful driving home. She locked everything up after he left and went back to the den to get Zep so that they could go to bed.

Chapter 12

The next few days went by with still no news on the girls. Wyatt hadn't gotten the DNA results back yet on the rope. On Friday morning, Landry went down to the lobby to wait on Ms. Millie to get there for them to go open the bookstore. Lisa saw her get off the elevator and stopped her.

"Hey, Landry. I have a favor to ask. Glenn moved his things from his old storage unit to his new one that is assigned to the two bedroom apartment that used to be Diane Huffman's. He said that she had left two boxes behind in the building and I was wondering if you would mind taking them to her this afternoon. I called the bank yesterday afternoon and they said she was off yesterday and again today. She took a couple of personal leave days to do some things at her house. I would take them, but my car is in the shop. Hannah dropped me off this morning and Jarred is going to pick me up this afternoon to run get my car. They close not long after I get off, so I was thinking maybe you could drop the boxes off at Diane's."

"Sure I can. Where does she live? Will she be expecting me?" Landry asked.

"She lives in that subdivision on the other side of the mountain that the hikers use. I have the address, but she has a hard time getting calls up there," Lisa explained.

"Oh, I know all about that. We never can get a signal when we go to the Sky High Tavern to eat. I guess it's all of those large mountains that interfere with the signal," Landry said and walked over to get a piece of paper and pen from Garrett's desk. "Just write down the address for me, and here's my key to my car." She took the car key off of her key ring. "Get Garrett to put the boxes in my car, and when I get off from the bookstore, I'll drop the boxes off to Diane. I have to go to the grocery store this afternoon anyway, so I can go to Diane's before I do that."

"Thanks, Landry. I'll let Glenn know that he and his wife can move their things to the storage unit tomorrow while she's in town. She's coming to visit for the weekend, and they'll be moving her things here the following weekend for her to stay permanently."

Ms. Millie came in the lobby and motioned for Landry to follow behind her to the bookstore. Landry winked at Lisa and made a face, then did exactly what Ms. Millie told her to. Lisa was laughing as they went out the door.

They had been at the bookstore for about two hours when Landry's phone rang. She saw it was Annie and she answered right away.

"How are things going there? I saw on the newscast last night that Penney is also missing now along with Jenna. Lan, I am so frightened for you." Annie got right to the point of her call.

"I'm fine, Annie. We make sure that none of us are alone in the bookstore and make sure we're looking over our shoulder at all times. There is some news. Adam and I went back up to Sky High Mountain to look around the crime scene and I literally fell into the rope that Wyatt thinks was used to kill Carla. He sent it off to the lab to check for DNA," Landry informed her.

"I pray Wyatt can figure all of this out soon. Did Ms. Millie get back alright from Mississippi?" Landry told her of the "bull incident" and by the time he was done with the story, Annie had gone from worried to laughing hysterically.

Landry looked out the office door and saw that Ms. Millie was helping a customer and had not heard her tell Annie the story. "It was funny," she said to Annie. "But, the part about my car running out of gas still bothers me. I know I had filled up before I left to pick her up at the bus station and Adam even took it to a mechanic to have it checked out. The mechanic said there was absolutely nothing wrong with the gas tank or the rest of the car."

"That's strange. I hope it doesn't happen again. How are Adam and Wyatt doing, anyway?" Annie asked.

"Wyatt is dog-tired from working so hard trying to figure out who kidnapped and killed Carla and who kidnapped Jenna and Penney and where they are. I do have some news on Adam, though. He's in a relationship with someone now," Landry said slyly.

"What? Who? I can't believe this. He looked like a puppy following you around when I was there. I was sure you guys would be together for a long time." Anne sounded shocked.

"Well, he's in a relationship with—me!" Landry laughed.

There was complete silence on the other end of the

phone. “Annie, are you still there?”

“I’m here. I can’t believe you did that to me. That was sneaky. But, I’m so happy for the two of you. I knew you were meant to be together.” She sounded very confident again.

“We’re taking it very slow. I love being around him, and truly can’t imagine being with anyone else. I’m trying to not get too excited, though. I want us to build a trusting, loving relationship and let it evolve in its own time.” Landry told her.

“Oh, Landry. Please just enjoy this time in your life. Don’t analyze it to death. Your new doctor seems to have found the right combination of medicine to help your anxiety. Don’t worry about the small stuff so much if you can help it. I have a very good feeling about you and Adam.” Landry could hear Annie smiling over the phone. She was always the romantic one of the two of them.

“By the way, have you seen Marston Hayes since I was there? I can’t believe I didn’t know he had a house in Bobwhite Mountain. That’s big, Landry. Why didn’t you tell me?” She pouted at Landry over the phone.

“I had no idea. There are several big celebrities who have built homes at the top of the mountain. They come here for peace, quiet and anonymity, so we rarely see them in town,” Landry told her.

“So, what’s going on with you? What’s up in Bent Branch?” Landry made herself a cup of coffee and sat down at the desk.

“It’s pretty busy here right now. We’re having the

annual fall celebration on the old railroad berm this weekend. We're busy today making goodies to sell at our tent tomorrow. The entire town and surrounding areas come out for it, as you know. This year, we have a few local bands that'll be playing and tons of tents and food trucks set up with fall vegetables and baked goods. The two main churches in town are hosting the hamburger/hot dog sales, and will be keeping the grills going. Mr. Conyers is doing his fried pork skins again, and several of the local ladies are selling crafts they've made throughout the year. It's a big time for us this weekend," Annie laughed. "And, it'll all end with a fireworks show at the football field."

At that moment, Landry had a feeling of homesickness. She loved it here in Bobwhite Mountain but she also had a flashback to when she and Annie were young and went to all the festivals and events together in Bent Branch. She had wonderful memories from her childhood. Living in a tiny town was boring sometimes, but the feeling of being able to walk anywhere in town and knowing everyone you ran into was a good one. She remembered when they were just small kids and their parents would take quilts or blankets to the high school football games. They would place them just outside the corner of the football field by the front end zone. The kids would play and have such a fun time. The fathers would stand in front of them facing the field to protect them from getting tackled or hit by a football. As they got older, their moms would drop them off at the school basketball games. They would get there early and watch the girl's and boy's games and their moms would pick them up afterwards.

She also remembered all of the sleepovers they had. Once, Landry had a birthday sleepover when she was a teen. They had all slept in her parents' camper in the side yard of her home. The highlight of the night was when the twin boys that lived a street over came to visit them in the camper. Landry's mom, Claire, had come out to bring extra blankets to them and found the guys sitting at the table in the camper. She escorted them back home and talked to their dad to be sure they didn't come back later that night. What fun memories…

"Landry! Landry, are you there?" Annie was yelling into the phone.

"Yeah, I'm here. The line must've messed up for a minute," she told Annie.

"A minute? You zoned out for a good three minutes. Don't even try to fool me. I'm your best friend, and I know when your attention is elsewhere. Did Adam walk in and you just couldn't speak for a minute?" Annie teased her.

"No. Honestly, I was just thinking about the fun we had growing up. You know, Bobwhite Mountain has a fall festival too. They hold it at the fairgrounds here and it's going to be tomorrow. Adam said there are lots of games, rides, food and fun. I can't imagine it even compares to Bent Branch's celebration, but I'm going to find out when I go tomorrow. The weather's wonderful here now. Perfect during the day and a little chilly at night. I really do love it." She heard Annie talking to a customer at the bakery.

"Whose attention is elsewhere now?" she laughed. "I'll

let you get back to work, Annie. I'll try to call you Sunday since we'll both be busy tomorrow. Love you."

"Okay. Love you, too." Annie hung up.

Landry heard the door open up front and looked up. It was Carter Morris, the fill in mailman. She gathered up the outgoing mail and took it to him. "How's Cecil doing? Has anyone spoken to him or Dinky lately?"

Carter put the mail in his bag and laid the incoming mail on the counter in front of Ms. Millie. "Oh, yeah. Our postmaster calls to check on him often. Dinky said that he's doing pretty good. She said his leg is healing nicely, but that the collar bone is giving him problems. She said he still can't walk very far and that when he goes back to the doctor, they'll see if the collar bone needs to be reset. It makes me hurt just thinking about it." He had a painful expression on his face.

"I'm sorry to hear that," Ms. Millie said. "Cecil's not a spring chicken. I was worried he wouldn't heal fast."

"Thanks for filling us in, Carter. I hope you have a good day," Landry told him.

The rest of the day went by fast. Landry got a lot of inventory done and organized the back office. Ms. Millie helped quite a few customers and told Landry that they'd made a good bit of money for the day already. When Maisy came into work after school, Landry waved at Sybil Penworth to let her know that she was waiting to let Maisy in the door. Maisy told her mom bye and walked in to get started on work.

Maisy asked Landry if the sheriff's department had

any leads yet in the case. Landry shook her head sadly and said, "I'm afraid not. I'm sorry, Maisy. This is hard for all of us but I know you are close to Jenna. Please just keep praying for her and Penney." She put her arm around Maisy's shoulder and tried to put a smile on her face. She felt so bad for Maisy. Landry kept thinking how horrible it would be if her best friend, Annie, went missing. She knew she would be inconsolable.

Landry told them she was leaving for the day and went back over to Magnolia Place to check on Zep and get her car. Josh Henley, the lobby assistant that came in at noon was holding the door open for Landry when she got there.

"Thanks, Josh." She turned to Lisa and asked if Garrett had placed the boxes for Diane in her car.

"He did. I texted you the address of her house. Did you get it?" Lisa asked her as she opened the bottom right hand drawer of her desk and took out a notebook to record something in.

As Landry was walking to the elevator, she said, "I sure did. Thanks, Lisa. I'm going to check on Zep and then head out. Adam's coming by later to take Zep for a walk, but I just want to be sure he's alright now."

She walked into the apartment and was just going to the den to check on Zep when there was a knock on her door. She turned around and thought how odd that was since Lisa normally buzzed up and let her know if someone was on the way up to see her. She looked through the peephole and was surprised to see James Larson standing there. She opened the door and said, "Hi, Mr. Larson." She was also surprised that he was standing there without a wheelchair or a walker.

"Hey, Landry. I was wondering if you had a few minutes for me to talk to you about something"

"Of course I do. Come on in." She held the door open for him.

"If you're busy, just say so. I can come back later," he told her.

"No, I'm not busy at the moment. I have a couple of errands to run but they don't have to be done at a certain time. Go back to the den and I will make us both some lemonade and bring it in there. We can talk while we drink it." She motioned the way for him to go down the hall.

She got the drinks and took them to the den. "Here you are. I don't know about you but I'm thirsty." She sat the drinks on the table between the recliner and the chair that he was sitting in, taking the recliner for herself.

"Now, what do you want to talk to me about?" she asked.

"Well, my physical therapist just left. As you can see, I'm walking and not in a wheelchair anymore. He had me do some exercises and get in and out of the shower for him and a few more things. Afterwards, he released me. He said I have healed up perfectly. The only restrictions are that I can't drive a car ever again and if I feel tired or faint, I can use my walker for a few weeks. Other than that, I'm free." He laughed.

"That's wonderful." Landry smiled. "I know you are pleased with the progress you made to heal so quickly. I'm sure Brad is happy, too," she said, speaking about Mr. Larson's son in Michigan.

"Oh, he is. The physical therapist actually called Brad from my apartment to tell him the good news. I think they are all surprised that I have done so well. Of course, Mary helped with that. She has taken great care of me. That's the other thing I want to speak to you about." He sipped some lemonade and petted Zep who had gotten into the chair with him.

Landry looked at him questionably and asked him to continue.

"Well, I have to tell Mary what the therapist said today. I know she is very fragile right now because of Penney missing and I don't want her to think that I just don't want her to come to see me anymore. That's not the case at all. I have enjoyed her company so much. In fact," he looked down at the floor, "I want to ask her to go out to dinner with me sometime. After Penney is found and back home, of course. What I wanted to ask you was if you think that's being too forward of me? I was married for many years and I haven't dated or spent time with any woman since my wife passed on. I don't want to do anything to disrespect Mary. She is a good woman, Landry."

She looked at him and smiled. "No, Mr. Larson. I don't think that will be disrespectful at all. You are both unattached and it will be good for the two of you to have someone to spend time with. As you said, after Penney is back home. I have been visiting with Mary and she isn't in a good place right now. I do, however, think she needs all of her friends around her right now. Maybe you could stop in to see her once a day–if that's ok with her, of course–to give her moral support and be a listening ear for her."

"I would love to do that. She has been so good to me and has taken such good care of me. We really have become friends. Thank you so much for taking the time to talk to me today, Landry. I think I will wait until tomorrow to give her the news about her not having to watch out for me anymore. Brad promised me that he would wait to call her for a couple of days until I could tell her myself. He also said that he was going to continue to pay her for the rest of the month until she could get another client scheduled to take my slot." He picked his glass up and said, "I'll just drop this off in the kitchen. I'll take my leave now so you can get to your errands."

Landry walked back to the living room with him and saw him out. She smiled to herself again and thought what a nice couple Mr. Larson and Mary Goode would make. She said a little prayer that Penney and Jenna would be home soon.

After she told Zep goodbye, she went back down to her car. She cranked it up and made sure there was still gas in it. She was in the habit of doing that since she still hadn't figured out what happened the night she and Ms. Millie ran out of gas. There had been no other problems at all since that night.

She plugged the address into her GPS and left the garage. The subdivision that Diane lived in was about thirty minutes away. It was on the other side of Sky High

Mountain at the top of the mountain. Landry was thinking it was a nice area when her GPS told her that she was where she needed to be. She pulled up into the driveway and got out of the Bug to reach back into the back seat and get the boxes. She was thinking that she should have brought Diane a housewarming gift when all of a sudden, she heard loud noises. Brakes screeching, sirens blaring and people yelling. She stood up and her mouth dropped open as she saw all of the law enforcement officers jumping from the cars and storming into the yard she was standing in. Out of the corner of her eye, she saw someone running towards her. She realized it was Wyatt.

"Landry, duck down behind your car door. Now!" he shouted at her. She did as he said and he knelt down beside her.

"What's going on, Wyatt? What in the world is happening?!" She was twisting her ring on her finger and gulping in air. She was frightened by all of this.

"We got the DNA back on the rope you found. It had Carla's DNA on it but they also found another one." Wyatt explained.

"Whose was it? Who killed Carla?" Landry asked as she twisted her ring to try to calm herself down.

Suddenly, they heard one of the deputies yell, "All clear, Sheriff."

Wyatt stood up and took Landry's hand to help her. Once she was up, she turned around and looked behind her to see what Wyatt was focused on. There, she saw Diane Huffman with handcuffs on. She had a deputy on each side of her, holding her arms.

Landry had a confused look on her face as she turned back to Wyatt. “Diane? Diane Huffman killed Carla?”

Wyatt nodded his head and said, “She did. At least I’m assuming she did, since the DNA belongs to her.” He waved one of his deputies over. “Make sure we comb this house from top to bottom. We still have two girls missing. Also, call Ben at the department. He stayed behind. Tell him to find Adam Wilcox. Ben has his number. Make sure to tell him that the first thing he should say to Adam is that Landry’s perfectly fine. Then tell Ben to go wherever Adam is and to bring him straight here. Adam can drive Landry back to town in her car.”

His deputy nodded and said he would get the message to Ben, and that they had already started combing the house inside and out.

Wyatt turned back toward Landry. “I don’t want to scare your boyfriend to death. That’s why I told Ben to make sure he tells Adam that you’re alright. I’ll wait here with you until they get here, and then I’m going back to the department to interview Diane. I want you and Adam to go back to your apartment and stay there. As soon as I get a break, I’ll come talk to both of you at the same time. I’m hoping by then I’ll have some news to give you about the girls.” He led Landry back over to her car.

As she got closer to the open door on her car, it hit her how blessed she was that she hadn’t gotten into Diane’s house before Wyatt and the others showed up. She could have been Diane’s next victim. She promptly lost her legs from beneath her and passed out.

When she woke up, Wyatt was standing there with a bottle of water in his hand and was waving a paper in front of her face. She realized he was fanning her face to try to wake her up. Landry sat up slowly and told him she was sorry that she'd passed out. She then expressed to him what she thought about right before she fell to the ground.

Wyatt looked at her and said, "I know. I think I lost a couple of years of my life when I rounded the corner and saw your car in front of Diane's house. I've never been so happy to see long, curly, red hair flying in the wind as I was when you popped your head up to see what was going on."

They smiled at each other and he looked behind her. "Here's your knight in shining armor. He's going to take you home now. I'll be by as soon as I can."

Wyatt helped her up and Adam took over. Wyatt told him that Landry would explain everything and that he'd see them later that night.

Chapter 13

They got back to the apartment and Adam took Zep for a walk. When they got back, Landry told him that she was going to make some grilled cheese sandwiches and some canned tomato soup. She was starving and she wanted comfort food. Adam agreed and made some sweet tea while she was cooking. He put down Zep's fresh food and water and then he and Landry sat down and ate.

"I have plenty of soup left for Wyatt and I'll make him a couple of sandwiches when he gets here," Landry told Adam as they got done eating and went outside on the balcony to sit in the crisp, autumn air. It felt good for her to breathe deeply and clear her senses from today.

"Why were you at Diane's anyway?" Adam asked as he took her hand in his.

She told him about the boxes Diane had left behind at Magnolia Place. Then she told him everything she could remember about what happened this afternoon. "I can't even imagine why Diane would have done this. It's just so horrible. Do you think she took the girls, too? Where could they be?"

Adam squeezed her hand and said quietly, "I have no idea. Let's just wait and see what Wyatt finds out. This is just so confusing to me, too."

They sat there and watched Zep play with his toys and waited to hear from Wyatt. It was almost two hours later before he showed up.

Adam opened the door for him and Landry told him that she had some food for him after he told them what he knew. She couldn't wait a second longer to hear what was going on.

Wyatt sat down on the couch and took a deep breath and let it out. "Here's what I know. This afternoon, before we got the DNA results on the rope, Jill Boatwright came to see me. She and her son, Les, got back from the Boy Scout trip today and Lenny told her that I needed to see her right away. She had some important information for me and she said that Diane had left the bank early last Friday, which we knew. She only worked a half day because she had a doctor's appointment to go to. We checked that out right away and found out that she did in fact go to the appointment." He stretched out and put his hands behind his head. Landry could tell he was tired.

"Jill said that before they left that day, Diane called back to the bank and spoke with Carla. She told her that she had left her purse in her desk drawer because she was in such a hurry to get to the doctor appointment. She told Carla that she knew she was leaving to go out of town right after work and asked her if she would mind dropping off her purse to her. Jill said they all knew where Diane's house was since they had given her a housewarming party the week before and everyone had gone to it. She said the only reason she knew what Diane had wanted when she called Carla is because Carla told her that she had to go get Diane's purse out of her office and also told her why." Wyatt asked Landry for a glass of tea and she got up to get it for him. She felt bad that she hadn't asked him if he wanted something to drink when he first got there, but she was itching to know what he had found out.

He thanked her and took a few sips of the tea before he continued.

"When I interviewed Diane, she didn't even want a lawyer present. As is the case with most first time criminals, she just wanted to get all the details off her chest. She said that when Carla got to her house, it was almost dark. She met her at the door with a pistol in her hand. Diane told Carla that they were going to take a walk. She blindfolded her so that Carla would be unable to fight back against her. She then took Carla's arm and they walked the long walk to the other side of Sky High Mountain. Diane said she didn't want to take the car since it would draw attention to them. Diane had worked at the tourist attraction on the mountain when she was in high school, way before the Pugh's bought it and built the Tavern. She knew exactly where that well was, since she was there when they closed it off and covered it. She had gone to the well site a few weeks ago and had opened it back up. She knew what she was going to do to Carla that far back." He shook his head and made a disgusted face. "After she killed her, Diane went back home and moved Carla's car to the back part of her property and covered it with tree limbs."

"Why did she want Carla dead?" Landry asked him.

"I'm getting to that. Anyway, she got them to the well and she hit Carla in the head with the butt of the pistol. It knocked Carla out but didn't kill her. Diane took the rope she had in her pocket and strangled Carla until she died. Then, Diane pushed her body into the well and covered it back up as best she could." He looked at Adam and said, "Premeditated murder. I can't understand some people." Adam nodded and told Wyatt to continue.

"It seems that not only was Carla seeing Kevin Dent, she'd also been having an affair with the bank manager before he left for another position at a different bank. See, Diane had been going to school at night for several years to get the education she needed to move up in the bank. She was positive that the bank manager position would be hers. Then, about a month ago, Carla started bragging within earshot of the others that she was applying for the bank manager position and that she was going to get it. Of course, the others laughed behind her back because the bank manager was leaving and they thought that the bank would choose a qualified person–they all thought that would be Diane–for the job. When Diane caught wind of what Carla said, she was livid. She had spent her entire adult life working at the bank and had moved up to assistant bank manager. She had just bought a new house because she was certain that her pay was going to almost double. She couldn't stand by and let Carla take it all from her. That's the reason she gave for killing her." Wyatt finished and excused himself to the bathroom.

While he was gone, Adam heated up some soup for him and Landry made him two grilled cheese sandwiches. Wyatt got back and sat down to eat.

"I hate to interrupt you while you're eating, Wyatt, but

what about the girls?" Landry asked and looked at him hoping he would have some good news.

"I'm sorry, Landry. Diane swears she had nothing to do with that and I believe her. I mean, she's going to prison for kidnapping and premeditated murder. Two more kidnapping charges wouldn't make a difference to her. She didn't kidnap Jenna and Penney." Wyatt looked truly sorry and sad about it.

"So, there's another person who took them. This is unbelievable," Adam said as he waved his arms around.

"It sure is," Wyatt said with a defeated tone. He finished his dinner and told them he had to get going. Adam reminded Wyatt that he didn't have his car and asked him if he could take him to it. Wyatt told him yes and told Landry that he would see her tomorrow at the fall festival at the fairgrounds. Adam bent down and gave Landry a kiss on the forehead and told her he would pick her up to go to the celebration around noon tomorrow.

"That would be great. I already told Ms. Millie that we aren't opening the bookstore tomorrow since everyone will be at the fall festival. I also told her that I'd pick her up so, if you don't mind, we can get her on the way there," Landry told him. He said that would be fine.

After they left, she turned everything off, made sure everything was locked up and she and Zep went to bed.

She said a prayer for Jenna and Penney. She prayed that they could stay alive and safe until someone could figure out where they were and rescue them. She turned out the light and closed her eyes.

When she woke up the next morning, Zep was still asleep. She looked at him and smiled. He was the cutest thing ever. If she could just manage to keep him away from cats, he would be pretty perfect. She heard his light snoring and left him there sleeping while she went to turn on the coffee pot.

She walked into the small office and called her mother. Landry hadn't talked to her in a while and wanted to be sure she was doing alright. The phone rang and rang with no answer. Landry left a message saying that she was just checking in and went back to the kitchen. There, she found an awakened Zep. She gave him fresh food and water and drank her coffee.

Landry did laundry, cleaned up the apartment and made a couple of lemon pies. She wanted to take those to Judith at the B&B after church tomorrow. Judith cooked every day for other people and Landry wanted to take her something just for her.

She saw on the weather channel that it was going to be unusually cool today, even for the mountains. She put on a long sleeved t-shirt, her jeans and a rust colored cardigan. She then slipped on her knee high boots and went down to Mary Goode's apartment to check on her before she went down to the lobby to wait on Adam.

Mary wasn't looking well. She was eating something, though, and Landry was glad for that.

"I made some canned soup and I'm trying to eat a little with crackers. Oh, Landry, I just want my Penney back home." Mary started crying.

Landry walked over to her and hugged her. "I know you do, Mary. I want her back home, too. I'm so sorry you have to sit here and wait to find out where she is."

"I saw on the news this morning that Diane Huffman was arrested for Carla's kidnapping and murder. I called Wyatt and he told me that Diane didn't kidnap the girls. I was disheartened in a way but in a way, I was glad. I mean, Diane killed Carla. Maybe the person who took the girls hasn't hurt them." Mary looked at Landry with hope in her eyes.

"That's my prayer, Mary. I pray they are found soon, unscathed and able to come back home." Landry told her comfortingly.

Mary told Landry that she had cleaned the apartment so much that her hands ached. She said she was trying to keep herself busy. Landry told her that was a good thing to do and that if she needed her for anything to just let her know. She left and went downstairs to the lobby.

"Hi, Orvis. How're things going with you?" She said as she walked into the lobby from the elevator.

"Just fine, Landry. I hope you aren't going out by yourself." He looked at her and shook his index finger at her like she had done something wrong.

"No. Adam's picking me up in a minute to go to the fall festival." She smiled at him.

She sat at Lisa's desk and while she waited, the retired cops started coming in the door for the event that Josh had scheduled. They were a great group of guys and Orvis told them to just go on up to the 5th floor. After they were out of earshot, he told Landry that the caterers had already been there and had put on a huge spread for the event.

It was just a few minutes until Adam pulled up. She got in the car and they went to pick up Ms. Millie. As she was getting in the car, Ms. Millie said, "Looka here, Landry. I don't want no foolishness from you today. I can't take being almost killed. You have got to leave me alone. You hear me?"

Landry rolled her eyes and said, "Ms. Millie, I don't ever try to get you hurt or killed. Those are coincidences that happen when we are together. Just sit back and enjoy the day. Nothing's going to happen."

Ms. Millie muttered something under her breath that sounded like, "I've heard that before. Lord, help me."

Adam grinned at Landry and drove them to the fairgrounds. The fall festival was already in full swing. They walked past the kiddie rides, apple bobbing, plastic ducks in the water and fishing games for the little ones. Landry remembered those from Bent Branch when she was little. She loved to put her fishing pole down behind the curtain and wait to feel that tug on the line. She would pull it up really fast and there would be candy on the end of the line. The kids were screaming with laughter at all the games.

Next were all the food trucks. There were corn dogs, cotton candy, candied and caramel apples, root beer that came in a glass bottle that looked like it was from decades ago but was new, fries with vinegar, funnel cakes, and so much more.

They came to a food truck that had fried shrimp and fries that they put in a paper cone. This truck also had the apple stack cake that Tennessee is famous for. They decided to walk around and come back later to get something to eat.

There was a huge tent set up for livestock and the judges were there judging who would win the blue ribbon later. The next game they saw was new to Landry. It was a human ring toss. People were sitting on chairs and the fair goers had to throw a hula hoop and try to get it around the body of one of the people. There were prizes like stuffed animals, insulated cups, costume jewelry and other trinkets to win.

The atmosphere was electric. Everybody was smiling and having fun. The coolness in the air was perfect and Landry saw many people that she knew. Ms. Millie was talking a mile a minute to everybody they met. Landry thought it was the happiest she had ever seen Ms. Millie. The live bands were playing at both ends of the fairgrounds.

Adam grabbed Landry's arm and told her to follow him. He said there was a game he always entered and he wanted to go there now. They got to a fenced-off part of a field towards the back end of the fairgrounds. There were blocks drawn on the grass inside the fence and they were all numbered.

"What's this for?" Landry asked him.

"Well, the game is called cow patty bingo. See, everyone who wants to play buys a ticket with a number on it that represents the blocks. Later today, they'll put a cow in the fence and whatever numbered block he ummm–does his business on–that's the winning number." Adam's enthusiasm got less and less as he explained it to her.

Landry stood there with her mouth dropped. "You mean–?"

"Yep. That's the gist of it." Adam bought his ticket and they walked away.

Landry was still shaking her head and laughing when Wyatt walked up to them. "Hey, guys. How's it going?"

"I was just explaining to Landry about cow patty bingo." Adam gave Wyatt a sideways smile. "I think she thinks I made the rules up."

Wyatt let out a loud laugh. "No, Landry, he didn't make it up. It's a real game and we have played since we were kids. In fact, I need to go buy my ticket before they all get bought up."

Landry just stared at them both in shock. She turned to Adam and said, "Where did Ms. Millie go?"

Adam turned around to see if he saw her and Wyatt said, "Oh, I saw her up at the cornhole games. She was beating the fire off our distinguished mayor." He grinned like it had made his day.

They walked around and checked out all of the exhibits and rides. Around four, Landry said that she was hungry. They all walked over to the food truck section. There was an empty picnic table there so Landry sat down to save it for them. She told Adam that she wanted the shrimp and fries and also a piece of apple stack cake. She had never had it, but everybody had told her it was delicious and she wanted to try it.

When the guys got back, they ate and waved to people they recognized. Of course, Adam and Wyatt knew everybody. Landry tried the apple stack cake.

“This is amazing,” she said between bites. “I love it.”

Wyatt smiled and told her, “That’s a cake that’s been famous in the Appalachian region for decades. I remember my grandma making it for us. She told me that it used to be served as a wedding cake and that guests would each bring a layer to the wedding and the women would then assemble it before the ceremony began.”

Wyatt’s radio went off a few times with his deputies checking in and letting him know everything was going good so far and that the only person they had to escort out was a young man that had gotten into the livestock area and tried to sit on a cow and ride it like a bull. Ben was the one to take him out of the fairgrounds and he told Wyatt that the man was highly inebriated. Ben ran the man home and told his wife to put him in bed and let him sleep it off.

It was getting to be dusk when Landry noticed everybody was assembling for the cake walk. She told Adam that she was entering that and since it was within eyesight of the cow patty bingo, he walked over there to watch the cow and see if he won. He kept his eyes on Landry at all times. She won a cake. He didn’t win bingo.

Wyatt and Ms. Millie walked up to them. Wyatt told Landry that he had to run to the department for a minute and would put the cake she won in Adam’s car for her.

Adam gave him his keys and thanked him.

Ms. Millie spoke up. “I’ve never been on a hayride. I’ve been watching them and they go real slow. I think I want to do that.”

Landry and Adam looked at each other and shrugged. “Sure, Ms. Millie. We’ll ride with you if that’s ok,” Adam said.

Adam helped Ms. Millie onto the trailer being used for the hayride and he and Landry hopped on. They were old school at the fairgrounds and used two horses to pull it instead of a tractor or truck. The horses started galloping slowly and they went all the way around the outside edge of the fairgrounds. It was getting downright cold now. Adam put his arm around Landry to keep the wind off of her. Ms. Millie had on her coat and had a scarf tied around her head. She looked like she was really enjoying herself. They got to the end of the ride and the driver stopped the horses. Everybody started getting off and Adam told Ms. Millie to wait and they would exit last so he could help her off.

As the others got off the trailer, Ms. Millie said, “That was nice. I liked that it was slow, and I enjoyed seeing all around the sides of the fairgrounds.” She and Adam started to walk towards the back of the trailer. Landry had gotten off and was waiting for them. Adam jumped down and turned around to take Ms. Millie’s hand.

Landry was looking out at the fairgrounds when she heard a couple of loud pops. She jumped and turned around to see that it was some kids popping balloons in the grass.

Ms. Millie was about to get off the trailer when it happened. The horses got spooked from the balloons popping. They both took off at full speed. That knocked Ms. Millie on her back and she shot off with the trailer flying down through the fairgrounds. Everybody started running after it, but the horses were too fast. Finally, the horses headed towards two big trees at the edge of the fairgrounds. They both went running between the trees, but the trailer was too wide. It got stuck between the trees and everything stopped. Several men ran to the horses to calm them down. Adam and Landry ran up to the trailer and all they saw was hay. Landry got tears in her eyes and said to Adam, "I did it this time. She must've flown out of the trailer. Adam, what if it killed her?"

Adam said, "No, Landry, she couldn't have done that. We were right behind the trailer the entire time." He looked back at the trailer and pointed. "Look!" There was a stack of hay that was moving.

He jumped into the trailer and started moving the hay around. When he got it cleared off, there she was. Ms. Millie was sprawled out under all that hay. Adam picked her up in his arms and started walking to the back of the trailer.

Landry heard a man behind her say, "What in tarnation is going on?" It was Wyatt. He had gotten back while all the commotion was happening. Adam bent down and handed Ms. Millie to Wyatt, who sat her gingerly on the ground.

"Ms. Millie, are you alright? We have EMT's here. Do

I need to get them to look at you?"

Ms. Millie looked straight at Landry and said, "No, Wyatt. I'm fine. Take me home."

"Look, Ms. Millie. You can't blame me for this one. You're the one who wanted to ride the hayride, not me. I didn't do anything to cause this." Landry stood her ground even though she was a nervous wreck just thinking about Ms. Millie being hurt.

Ms. Millie looked at Adam. "Take me home. Now."

Wyatt helped Ms. Millie up and Landry saw something shiny on her coat. She walked over to see what it was and Ms. Millie jumped back. "Don't touch me, Landry. I mean it."

Landry rolled her eyes and told her that she just wanted to see what was on her coat. She reached down and caught in the cuff of the coat there was a bracelet. Landry pulled it out and she and Ms. Millie both made an O formation with their mouths. Their eyes were big as saucers.

"Ms. Millie, I think you need to ask for forgiveness tomorrow at church for accusing your grandson of being a hardened criminal." Landry turned around and headed to Adam's car.

They got Ms. Millie back home and told her goodbye. She told them that she wasn't going to church tomorrow, so don't come by to get her. She said she was going to call Vanessa and tell her what had happened. She also said she was going to go online and order Wesley a nice gift to send to him.

When they got back on the road, Adam asked Landry what was going on and she told him the whole sordid story. "I kept telling Ms. Millie the bracelet would show up and that I just didn't believe that Wesley had taken it. I know she's upset that she even thought that."

Adam nodded his head. "I really am glad she found it. It had to be hard on her to think that he would've done that to her."

"Oh, by the way," Landry said to him. "I'll be driving my own car to church tomorrow. I know you have that meeting with the rest of the men of the church after services and while you are doing that, I think I'm going to take that butterscotch cake that I won in the cake walk to Dinky and Cecil. I know Dinky has to have been running herself ragged with Cecil's needs. I won't go in since I don't want to intrude. I'll just hand it to her on the porch. Then, I made your mom a couple of lemon pies and I want to drop those off to her. By the time I do all of that, you should be done at your meeting and we can go out to eat if that's ok with you."

"Sounds good to me. I really don't want you to be out by yourself, though. Until we figure out who kidnapped the girls and they're back home safe, I worry about you being alone." Adam pulled his car into Landry's parking garage. He got out and opened her door and got the cake off the backseat to carry in.

"I know but Dinky and Cecil live in town. From what Lisa told me, they live right down the street from Wyatt. And, there will be people at the B&B and I can call your mom on my way so that she will be looking for me," Landry argued.

Adam sighed. "Alright. I can't make you do what I think is best. Just keep your head on swivel and be aware of your surroundings."

"I will. I promise," she said. They had gotten to the door of her apartment and went inside. Zep was there waiting for them and started yelping and spinning in circles when he saw Adam. Zep was a smart dog and he knew Adam had been the one to take him on walks lately. Adam laughed and got the leash.

"We'll be back," he said as they walked out of the door. Landry smiled and put the cake in the fridge until tomorrow. Her phone rang at that moment. She looked down at the caller ID and answered.

"Hi, Mom. How are things going with you?" she asked Claire.

"Alright, I guess. I hurt my back while I was walking down some steep stairs and the doctor gave me some medicine that makes me so sleepy. I've been sleeping the days away and I don't like it one bit. How are you doing?" Claire sounded depressed.

Landry debated on telling her mother everything that was going on at the moment in Bobwhite Mountain. Her mother was convinced this was a terrible town and that Landry should run away from it as fast as she could. On the other hand, she knew that if her mother heard about all of the happenings from someone else first, she would never hear the end of it.

She took a deep breath and told Claire everything about finding Carla's body, who her killer was and also about the girls being kidnapped. She braced herself for her mother's outburst.

But something strange happened. Claire just said, "Ok, dear. Just please be careful. I have to go lay back down now. Call me with any news." Claire hung up.

Landry stood there, staring at the phone. Had someone kidnapped her mother, too. Were they standing there telling her what to say? She finally decided that it must be the medicine Claire was on. She would call again tomorrow and check on her.

Adam brought Zep back and left for home. Landry found what she would wear to church tomorrow and laid it out on the bed in the spare bedroom. She got a nice, hot shower and she and Zep went to bed. Before she started reading some, she prayed. This time, not only for the girls and their families but also for her mother. She had a feeling that her mother needed special prayers tonight. She read for about half an hour and then turned out the lamp and went to sleep.

Chapter 14

She woke up the next morning and had a cup of coffee and a bagel for breakfast. Zep ate his own breakfast and went to lay back down in the den. She called Ms. Millie to check on her.

"What is it, Landry?" was how Ms. Millie answered her phone.

Landry sighed and said, "I was just calling to make sure you're alright."

"Other than being sore and ashamed, I'm fine'" Ms. Millie told her.

"Ms. Millie, don't be ashamed. You didn't actually tell anyone what you suspected about Wesley except for me. None of the family will ever know." Landry tried to console her.

"I know you're right, but I still feel guilty for even thinking about it. You told me the entire time that it would show up and that Wesley was not the kind of boy to do that. I want to thank you for that, Landry. You had more confidence in my grandson than I did. That means a lot to me that you think so highly of my daughter and her family." Ms. Millie sounded properly put in her place. This was an unusual circumstance for Landry. She didn't quite know how to respond.

"You're welcome, Ms. Millie. It was easy for me to believe that. You see, they all come from great stock. You are the salt of the earth. Like Aunt Tildie always said, 'the apple doesn't fall far from the tree'," Landry told her. "I have to get ready for church now. Are you sure you don't want me to pick you up?"

"No, not today. I have some meditating to do on my own today. I'll see you at the bookstore in the morning." Ms. Millie hung up.

Landry got ready and put the butterscotch cake in an insulated cake carrier. It sure did look good. She hoped that Dinky and Cecil would enjoy it. She also put the lemon pies in the other insulated container.

After church, she told Adam that she would see him later. He said that he'd wait in the church parking lot for her after the meeting and follow her back to her apartment. He told her that he was thinking that they might go over to Wrigley Springs to the Mexican restaurant that everybody raved about and then stop by the farm on the way home and visit with Steve and Denise. That sounded wonderful to Landry.

She got to Dinky and Cecil's house and got the cake out of the backseat. She walked up on the porch and knocked. No one came to answer it. She knocked again, this time harder. She listened and finally, after a few minutes, she heard footsteps. Dinky opened the door. She had on her apron over her clothes and was wringing her hands. She looked upset.

"Hi, Dinky. Is something wrong?" Landry asked her.

"Oh, Landry. I can't believe it's you. You showed up at the perfect time. Cecil has started walking a little now, and he decided this morning that he would try to walk to the kitchen and back to the bedroom. He got in here alright but started to stumble. He fell against the basement door and I hadn't closed it tightly. He fell, and down the stairs he went. I can't get him up by myself. Can you help me?" Dinky looked like she was at the end of her rope.

"Of course, Dinky. Let me sit this cake down. I brought it to you and Cecil." Landry put the cake on the counter and went to the basement door. She started down the steps, with Dinky right behind her.

"Oh, let me turn the stairway light on so you can see better." Dinky went back to turn on the light.

The next sound Landry heard was the basement door slamming and being locked. She stood there in the dark in shock. She yelled up the stairs, "Dinky, the door closed behind you. Please hurry and turn on the light. I don't want to trip over Cecil."

Nothing. Not one word from Dinky. Landry slowly walked down the basement stairs. When she got to the bottom, a faint light came on. Once her eyes adjusted, she couldn't believe what she saw. The light was from a tiny lamp that was inside a huge cage. It actually looked like the largest dog kennel she had ever seen. Inside the kennel, there was Jenna and Penney. Penney jumped up and said, "Landry. Thank the Lord you found us! I have been praying so hard for someone to find us." She started crying and shaking.

"Penney, what's going on? Did Dinky and Cecil kidnap the two of you?" At that moment, Lisa's face popped into Landry's mind. She remembered the day Lisa had shown her the fliers of the girls and had pointed out how much alike they looked. Like twins. She knew exactly what was going on.

"Not Cecil," Penney told her. "In fact, we haven't even seen him since Dinky brought us here. She's crazy, Landry. I mean she has mental issues. Dinky dresses us up in the exact same outfits. She hands them between the bars to us and makes us put them on. She calls us 'Bailey and Hailey'. Jenna said that was her and Cecil's twin girls' names. Jenna also said that she had seen a picture of them and they were slim like us and had long blonde hair like us. I think Dinky thinks we're them."

"I wonder how Dinky constructed this cage thing in the basement?" Landry was actually thinking out loud, but Penney answered her.

"When she put us in here the first time, she said, 'This comes in nicely to keep you girls safe. Good thing your father had it built down here to put the chickens in when there was a tornado headed this way'. I guess Cecil didn't want his chickens to get killed in a tornado." Penny shrugged.

Landry noticed Jenna hadn't moved while Penney was talking. "What's wrong with Jenna? Is she sick?" she asked Penney.

"Jenna's a diabetic. I thought you knew. She hasn't had her medicine in over a week. She's very sick. I'm so worried about her. I'll tell you everything else but, please get us out of here," Penney pleaded.

"I wish I could, Penney. I stumbled upon you. I had no

idea you were here. Dinky told me that Cecil had fallen down the stairs and was down here. Then she slammed the door and locked me in." Landry reached in her back pocket for her cellphone. It wasn't there. She remembered when Dinky had been walking right behind her on the stairs. She must have taken the phone.

"How do you two use the bathroom here?" Landry knew it was a stupid question but she was trying to get Penney's mind off of the current situation.

Penney walked to the back of the cage and showed Landry where Dinky had put a bedside toilet behind a curtain. "She empties it when she comes down to 'play' with us. She makes us play little children's games with her. She also has a gun that she points at us so that we won't try to jump her. She chains our wrists to the metal bars on the cage so that she can change our bedclothes and dump the toilet in the real bathroom over there." Penney pointed at a door.

Landry got sick to her stomach. What these girls had been through was horrible. She decided she didn't want to ask any more questions. She couldn't take the answers. Her main concern now was trying somehow, someway to get into the cage with the girls and get them out. She was worried about Jenna. She sent up a prayer thanking the Lord that they were still alive. She had to figure out how to get out of this place.

The only window was way up almost to the ceiling. It was so small she doubted she could get through it to escape and get help, even if she could figure out how to get up there. She looked around the basement until she found a thin piece of metal. She tried and tried to break the lock on the cage but it wouldn't budge. When she finally gave up, she had cut her fingers up so much that she was bleeding pretty bad. Penney handed her a washcloth that was on her bed. "It's clean. Dinky makes sure everything is clean here."

Landry put it on her fingers and went to the bathroom in the basement. She washed her hands and wrapped the washcloth around them. She went back out and sat outside the cage. "When's the last time Jenna was awake, Penney?"

"Earlier this morning. Dinky brought us breakfast and sang us hymns. Jenna ate a small amount and then laid back down. She went to sleep and hasn't been awake since. Landry, I'm scared she's going into a coma." Penney was shaking all over.

"Please calm down, Penney. I need you to be calm so that maybe we can think of some way to get out of here." Landry knew it was next to impossible but she really needed Penney to calm down. As it was, Landry was spinning her ring and trying her best to not have a panic attack. Every time she looked at Jenna, she felt like she was going to pass out from fear for her.

She remembered something at that moment. She looked at Penney and said, "I told Adam where I was going. He knows I was headed here. Hopefully, after they realize I'm missing, they'll come here and find us. I just hope Jenna can hold on." Landry knew her face had to show how worried she was for Jenna.

Penney gave her a sad look and said, "Unfortunately, even if they do come here, they would have to know to come down here to find us. When we first got here, Jenna and I yelled and yelled, hoping someone would hear us. Dinky told us that this basement was completely soundproof. She said Cecil made sure of it since 'we' played our music so loud when we were teens. It has been like we fell down the rabbit hole, Landry. I honestly thought I was losing my mind for a while. She calls us by her twin daughters' names and when I tried to reason with her and tell her our real names, she got so angry and told me that she didn't raise me to talk back to her."

Penney had tears in her eyes and asked Landry, "How is my Mom doing? I know she has to be so worried."

Landry told her that her mom was holding up and that everyone was there for her when she needed them. She also told Penney that Mary was certain she was still alive and would come home.

Penney dropped her head and said, "She told me not to jog anymore until they found out who kidnapped and killed Carla and who kidnapped Jenna. I should've listened to her." She jerked her head back up and her eyes were big. "Landry, we haven't seen Carla while we've been here. Do you think Dinky put her somewhere else or something?"

Landry sighed heavily as she told Penney that Carla was taken by someone else. She told her who and why and that Carla was killed. She hated to tell Penney that but she didn't want to lie to her and at least it gave them something to talk about while they waited for someone to come find them.

"Penney, how did Dinky kidnap you? Did Jenna tell you how Dinky got her?" Landry asked.

"With me, it was my stupidity. I was inside the park jogging. There were even other people around so I felt safe. After my second lap, Dinky came running up to me and she was frantic. She said that she had taken Cecil to the doctor and then they decided to go eat out. She said she put Cecil in the back of the van in his wheelchair when they got done. She told me that as she was driving, the wheelchair turned over with Cecil and he was lying in the back of the van moaning and that she must have not locked the wheelchair in like she was supposed to. She said it was a rental handicap van she got so that she could get Cecil to his doctor appointments. Anyway, she begged me to come help her get Cecil up. Of course I took off running with her to the van." Penney looked sick to her stomach just telling Landry the story.

"Dinky came into the boutique all the time and I knew her, so I didn't even think about it. When we got to the van, she told me that the latch on the back door was broken and that she had to put Cecil in through the side door. She said I would have to get in the side door and walk to the back to get him up. She slid the side door open and I stepped in. Just as I realized Cecil was nowhere in the van, I felt a cloth over my mouth and nose. I guess it was chloroform or something. You know, Dinky was a nurse for years. When I woke up, I was so drowsy and she was walking me down the basement stairs. I have no idea how she got me that far.

I mean, she is so tiny and I am so tall. I guess I was in that twilight phase and was just doing what she told me. I saw Jenna when I got down here." Penney's voice got as low as a whisper as she finished the story.

"Oh, Penney. Don't feel stupid. I would have done the exact same thing. Who on earth would have suspected that Dinky was capable of kidnapping?" Landry held her hand through the metal bars of the cage. "Did Jenna tell you how Dinky got her?"

"Yeah. Basically, the same way. She said that Dinky rang the back doorbell at the bookstore and Jenna put the sign up in the window, locked the front door, went to the back office and checked to make sure it was a delivery driver that she knew. She saw it was Dinky and that she was holding up two books. Jenna said that you had sent the books to Cecil, and that you had told Dinky to return them for other books if he'd already read them." Penney turned to look at Jenna's sleeping figure as she told the rest of the story.

"When Jenna opened the door, Dinky said the same thing to her that she did to me. Of course, Jenna told her she would help Cecil. Jenna went to the van and, as she got in, Dinky put the cloth over her mouth and nose and brought her here. Jenna told me that she was sorry that I was kidnapped, too, but that she was glad that I was here with her." Penney walked over to the cot Jenna was on and took her hand. She said a prayer that someone would find them in time. Afterwards, she put her face in her hands and bawled.

Landry was doing her breathing exercises and was reaching for her ring when she heard the doorknob shaking on the door at the top of the stairs. She put her finger to her mouth and told Penney to be quiet. She ran over to the bottom of the staircase and got back as far as she could, hoping that she could surprise Dinky and tackle her as she stepped off the last step. It was their only chance.

She heard the door burst open and footsteps coming down into the basement. She was poised to jump when Penney yelled, “Wait, Landry! It’s Sheriff Collins!”

She looked over and saw Wyatt. She ran to him and hugged him tight. She looked towards the heavens and said, “Thank you, Jesus!” Then she grabbed Wyatt and said, “Jenna’s a diabetic and hasn’t had her meds in a long time. She needs to get to the hospital now! It might already be too late.”

As she heard him call upstairs on his radio telling them about Jenna, she saw two deputies come down the stairs with hacksaws. They got the bars cut open in no time flat. Penney rushed out and threw her arms around Landry. She then looked at Wyatt and told him that she feared that Dinky had done something bad with Cecil since she hadn’t seen him the whole time she’d been there. The three of them were walking up the stairs just as the EMT’s were coming down with a stretcher for Jenna.

“How’d you find us, Wyatt?” Landry questioned him as they stepped out of the way.

“When you didn’t show up when Adam thought you should’ve, he called Judith and asked her if you had gotten there. She told him that she hadn't seen you, so, since he knew you planned to stop here first, I grabbed my deputies and we came here. Adam took his car and tried to backtrack the route you should've taken to be sure your car hadn't run out of gas again and left you stranded. When I got here and saw your car, I had a deputy text him. He should be here soon." Wyatt turned to finish walking up the stairs but stopped and said, "We banged on the front door, but Dinky never came. We knocked even harder and I was yelling for her to come to the door. When she still didn't come, I ordered my deputies to bust the door down. I yelled at her when we got in and asked where you were. She cracked and said that you and the girls were in the basement and that she was sorry but that she wanted to spend some time with the twins. I knew then what was going on and I came straight down here. My deputies finished arresting her." He, Landry and Penney all started up the stairs again.

When they got to the top, one of Wyatt's deputies stood in the doorway. He said, "Sheriff, you need to come with me. There's something you need to see."

Wyatt turned to follow him and asked him, "Where's Dinky? Is she in custody?"

"Yes sir. She's in the back of a car and headed to the department with Cora. She had a gun in her apron, but when we busted in, she seemed to just deflate and gave up after she told you that Miss Burke and the girls were in the basement. She keeps asking if her twins are alright. She says that they are only sixteen and that someone needs to be with them while she's away."

He looked at Wyatt intently. "She said their names are Bailey and Hailey. Sheriff–" he started to say something. Wyatt cut him off and said, "I know, Tyler. I know." He shook his head and followed his deputy to the back part of the house.

Tyler led him to a back bedroom. There, Wyatt saw Cecil. He looked terrible. The second set of EMT's were working on him. Tyler told him, "When we found him, he was chained to the bed. The EMT's say that it looks like he never went back to the doctor after they put the casts on him when he fell and broke his collarbone and leg. We asked Cecil if he's been eating, and he said that Dinky brought him food once a day, but that he has a hard time feeding himself. He also told us that she forced him to use the bedpan, and that he's not walked or been out of this bed since she put him in it the first day he came home. He had no idea about the girls being in the basement. I'm assuming that Dinky chained him up so he wouldn't find out about the girls and call someone."

Wyatt and Tyler looked at each other in disbelief and disgust. "How on earth could she be so nuts that she could do this to her own husband? Not to mention kidnapping and holding two young girls hostage." Wyatt shook his head and went back to the living room while the EMT's carried Cecil out on the stretcher. They took him and Jenna to the hospital. After the EMT's cleared Penney, Landry asked Wyatt if she could take her home to her momma. He nodded and told Penney that he would have to interview her the next day. On the way out, Landry grabbed the butterscotch cake and handed it to him. “Take this with you so you and the deputies will have a snack while you’re working.”

Wyatt looked grateful and took the cake.

“I feel bad for Dinky, Wyatt. She obviously never dealt with the death of her twins. I wish she had reached out for professional help to help her cope. I think when I knocked on the door, she panicked. She probably thought that if she didn’t answer the door, I would get someone to make a welfare check on her and Cecil since her car was in the driveway. I’m sure she also thought that I would insist on speaking to Cecil, even just to say hello. She couldn’t let me do that because she had him chained to the bed.” Landry shook her head.

As they were all walking out to the vehicles, Adam pulled up and jumped out of his car almost before it had stopped. He ran up to Landry and held her for a long time. Then he grabbed Penney and hugged her. Landry told him to follow her home and that she was taking Penney with her.

On the way home, Penney broke down. She cried and cried. She told Landry that she had been so worried that she would never see her Mom again. It broke Landry’s heart.

“Well, you’re going to see her in just a few minutes, Penney. I just want to let you know how proud I am that you stayed so brave and did whatever crazy things Dinky asked you to do in order to keep yourself and Jenna alive until someone could find you.” Landry reached over and squeezed her hand.

Chapter 15

Landry and Penney stood at Mary's door. Landry looked at Penney and asked if she was ready. Penney nodded.

Landry knocked and Mary answered. She looked so sad and Landry could tell she had been crying. She motioned for Landry to come in.

"I'll come in, Mary, but only if you let my friend come in with me." Landry stood to the side and Penney walked up. Mary grabbed the doorframe and almost fell. Landry reached to help steady her.

"My baby! My baby is back with me!" Mary screamed. Penney ran to her and they hugged each other and cried for several minutes. When they started inside, Mary looked back at Landry. "Come in."

"No, Mary. You two need time to yourselves. Penney will tell you the whole story and she has to go to see Wyatt tomorrow to give her statement. Go celebrate and, if I can ask, please say a prayer for Jenna. She's very sick." Landry turned and went to the elevator, knowing that the two women would be fine now.

When she got to her apartment, Adam was sitting on the floor by her door with the lemon pies that she had intended to take to Judith. He had his head in his hands and his elbows on his knees. He heard her get off the elevator, stood up and picked up the container with the pies. He reached for her keys and opened the door. He put his arm around her and walked her into the apartment. Zep greeted them with yelps and spins. Adam told her to please sit down and rest until he and Zep got back from their walk. After she put the pies in the refrigerator, she went to the couch and sat down. It hit her in that moment that she would be able to walk Zep alone again just like they used to before all the kidnappings in town. She was glad that Bobwhite Mountain could get back to the quaint, peaceful mountain town that she loved.

When Adam and Zep got back, they all went into the den and sat down. Adam had gotten Zep some of his treats and refilled his water bowl. Zep wasn't having any of it. Somehow, he knew Landry had been through a lot earlier in the day and he jumped onto the sofa with her. He wiggled and moved around until he was right next to her leg. He let out a big sigh and went to sleep.

Adam's phone rang and he told her it was Wyatt. He answered and put it on speaker phone. Wyatt said, "I don't have much time since I'm still working the investigation but I wanted to let you guys know a few things I've learned. The doctors think Jenna is going to be alright. The ER docs said that she was very near death when the EMT's got to her, though. They are working on her and giving her medicines and fluids. They'll be keeping her for several days to be sure. Her folks are with her now."

Landry could hear papers crinkling in the background. Wyatt continued, "Dinky is certifiable. Since she didn't kill anyone, she will go to the psych ward for evaluation. Just from talking to her myself, I figure she will be there permanently or at least until a good therapist can straighten out her mind. You know, I always thought it was Cecil that couldn't move on without their twin girls; I was wrong. He was coping as best he could and Dinky had everyone thinking that she was the one who was doing fine." Wyatt sounded sad and confused about all of it.

Landry said, "That just goes to show that we never know what someone is going through on the inside. Some people hide it very well–until they don't. It's so sad."

Wyatt replied in a low, gravelly voice, "Don't I know it. I know all about grief and how it can tear you apart. Most people can get past it at least enough to live normal lives. Some can't process it and eventually, it eats them up." Landry knew Wyatt was talking from experience.

He cleared his throat and continued. "Cecil's going to surgery in a couple of days. They said his leg's healing up, but that the collarbone was messed up badly. They want to get some nutrition and fluids in him before they do the surgery, though. I spoke to him at the hospital and he's still in a state of shock over all that's happened. I told them to put me down as his next of kin in case of an emergency, since he has no other relatives. That's about all I have for now–oh, one more thing. I called over to the bus station in Wrigley Springs and asked them to send me camera footage of the back parking lot from the day you picked up Ms. Millie, Landry."

Wyatt answered a question that someone came in and asked him about before he went on. "Anyway, the footage came in while I was out there at Dinky and Cecil's house. Cora checked it when she got back here. I solved your mystery. It seems that when you went to meet the bus and while you and Ms. Millie were arguing over you dumping her clothes out in the parking lot and then you were fussing at her for saying whatever she said to the nice fellow that was going to help pick them up, there was a sleazebag in the back parking lot siphoning your gas out. Nobody else was back there since they had also gone up front to meet the bus. He worked fast and was out of there before any of you got back to the lot. Wrigley Springs picked him up and arrested him for it. I guess he left enough in the car for you to get as far as the farm before you ran out." Wyatt answered his other line and said, "Sorry, gotta run."

"Well, I guess that solves that. I'm glad there wasn't anything wrong with my car but, I do feel violated that someone could just take the gas out of my car without me knowing it." Landry told Adam.

She smiled and replied, "I'll try to be more careful in the future. Although, I thought I was being careful today. I'm just glad it's over and that the girls are alive and safe. Now–" she was interrupted by a knock on the door.

She went to answer it, with Adam right behind her. She opened the door and stood there in complete shock. Her mouth dropped open. Adam looked at her and immediately knew that something was wrong. He picked up the pace and was by her side looking at a woman he had never seen before in his life.

Landry finally got her mouth to work and said, "Mother. What are you doing here?"

Claire sashayed into the apartment, looked Adam up and down and said, "What a way to greet your mother,

Landry. I'm visiting you for a while. My driver's bringing my things up. Which bedroom should I take?"

Landry and Adam looked at each other. It felt like the temperature in the apartment dropped 20 degrees. Landry could only imagine what the coming weeks had in store.

THE END

RECIPES

THREE INGREDIENT PUMPKIN COOKIES

Ingredients:
1 box of spice cake mix
1 can of pumpkin puree
1 cup milk chocolate chips

Mix all ingredients together in a large bowl. Roll into tablespoon sized balls and place on an ungreased baking sheet.

Bake at 375 degrees for 12-25 minutes. Do not overcook.

Enjoy!!

PINWHEEL ROLL-UPS

Ingredients:
½ pound deli sliced ham, chopped up
1 cup mild shredded cheddar cheese
1 block cream cheese, softened
1 packet of ranch seasoning mix
1 green onions, chopped small
Flour tortillas

Mix together chopped ham, cheese, cream cheese, ranch seasoning, and green onions.

Spread an even layer of the mixture onto each flour tortilla.

Roll up the tortillas into long log shapes.

Wrap all of the tortillas separately in foil and put in the refrigerator overnight.

The next day, cut the rolled up tortillas in 1 inch intervals to make the pinwheels.

(Landry says that you can also add black olives or green/red peppers if you chop them up finely.)

LUNCH LADY SPAGHETTI

Ingredients:
1 16oz box of angel hair pasta noodles
1 24oz jar of marinara sauce
1 lb COOKED ground beef, seasoned
4 cloves of garlic, minced (not a typo)
2 tablespoons olive oil
¼ tsp salt
¼ tsp black pepper
¼ tsp Italian seasoning
1 cup shredded mozzarella cheese
Water

Preheat the oven to 400 degrees.

Cook ground beef and put it to the side.

Place the UNCOOKED noodles evenly at the bottom of a casserole dish. (Landry says that if you need to, you can break these in half.)

Pour the marinara sauce over the noodles and spread evenly with a spatula.

Sprinkle the COOKED ground beef, garlic, olive oil, salt, pepper and Italian seasoning on top of the marinara sauce.

Pour enough water in to cover everything completely.

Gently mix everything together in the casserole dish and put in the oven.

Bake at 400 degrees for 25 minutes.

Take the spaghetti out of the oven and stir to unstick any noodles that might be stuck together.

Sprinkle the mozzarella cheese on top.

Put back in the oven and let it cook until the cheese is golden brown on top.

Take it out, let it cool for 10 minutes. Enjoy!

BUTTERSCOTCH CAKE

Ingredients for cake:
2½ cups all purpose flour
3.4oz butterscotch instant pudding mix
3½ tsp baking powder
½ tsp salt
¾ cup unsalted butter, room temperature
1½ cups packed light brown sugar
3 tablespoons vegetable oil
1 tsp vanilla
4 large eggs
1¼ cups milk

Ingredients for frosting:
1¼ cups unsalted butter, room temperature
11oz butterscotch chips, melted
6¼ cups powdered sugar
½ tsp salt
½ cup milk or cream

Directions for Cake:

Preheat the oven to 350 degrees.

Prepare 3 8 inch cake pans with parchment paper circles in the bottom of the pans and grease the sides.

Combine flour, pudding mix, baking powder and salt in a medium sized bowl and set to the side.

Combine butter, brown sugar and vegetable oil in a large mixing bowl and beat together until light and fluffy, about 3-4 minutes. DO NOT skimp on the creaming time.

Add the eggs and vanilla extract and mix until completely combined and smooth. Scrape down the sides of the bowl as needed to be sure all ingredients are well incorporated.

Add half of the dry ingredients to the batter and mix until mostly combined.

Add the milk and mix until well combined. The batter will look a little curdled, but that's okay.

Add the remaining dry ingredients and mix until well combined and smooth. Scrape down the sides of the bowl as needed to be sure all ingredients are well incorporated. Do not over mix the batter.

Divide the batter evenly between the cake pans and bake for 22-25 minutes, or until a toothpick comes out with a few crumbs.

Remove the layers from the oven and allow to cool for about 2-3 minutes, then move to the cooling racks to completely cool.

Directions for frosting:

Add butter to a large mixing bowl and beat until smooth.

Slowly add the melted butterscotch chips and mix until combined.

Add half of the powdered sugar and mix until smooth.

Add the remaining milk or cream as needed to get the right consistency. Set this to the side.

To put cake together:

Use a large serrated knife to remove the domes from the top of the layers so that they are flat. Place the first layer on top of a plate or cardboard cake round.

Spread about 1 cup of the frosting into an even layer on top.

Add the second layer on top of that and spread another cup of frosting on that.

Put the last layer on top and put the remaining frosting on the top and sides of the cake.

Press butterscotch chips into the sides of the cake immediately after frosting it.

Store in an airtight container. Best when eaten in 3-4 days.

*Landry admits that this cake takes more time than most but says that it is absolutely worth it.

TENNESSEE STACK CAKE

Ingredients:
1 cup plus 2 tablespoons unsalted butter, divided
1½ cups sugar
3 large eggs
5 cups all purpose flour
1 tablespoon baking powder
½ tsp salt
½ tsp apple pie spice
2 cups whole buttermilk
¾ cup molasses
½ tsp vanilla
½ cup honey
2 cups sweetened whipped cream
Apple filling

To make cake:
Preheat the oven to 350 degrees.
Grease and flour 3 9 inch round cake pans.
In a large bowl, beat 1 cup of the butter and the sugar with a mixer on medium speed until fluffy.
Add eggs one at a time, beating well after each one.
In a medium bowl, whisk together flour, baking powder, salt and the apple pie spice.
In a small bowl, whisk together the buttermilk and molasses.
Gradually add flour mixture to butter mixture

alternately to the buttermilk mixture, beginning and ending with the flour mixture. Beat just until combined after each is poured in.

Stir in vanilla.

Pour the batter into the layer pans.

Bake until a wooden toothpick that is inserted into the center of each comes out clean (about 30 minutes).

Take out of the oven and let cool for 10 minutes in the pans.

Remove layers from pans and let them cool completely on wire racks.

After cool, cut each of the layers in half horizontally to make them thin

To make the apple filling:

3 packages of dried apples (4.5oz each)

3 cups water

2 cups sugar

¼ cup unsalted butter

2 tablespoons molasses

3 tsp apple pie spice

Combine all ingredients in a medium saucepan and bring to a boil.

Let boil for 2 minutes and then remove from heat and let cool completely.

Put in a food processor and pulse 5 to 6 times until coarsely chopped.

To assemble cake:

Put apple filling between the layers that you cut in half (so they are thin) as you put them on a cake plate or cardboard cake round.

Heat honey and remaining 2 tablespoons of butter over medium heat until butter is melted.

Brush the cake with the honey mixture and top with whipped cream.

LANDRY'S EASY LEMON PIE

Ingredients:

1 block of cream cheese, softened
⅓ cup lemon juice
1 can sweet condensed milk
1 graham cracker crust
Fruit of your choice

Put softened cream cheese in a mixer bowl. Beat on high until creamy.

Pour in condensed milk and lemon juice and mix until everything is combined.

Pour into a prepared graham cracker crust and refrigerate for at least an hour.

*Landry says that you can top this with your favorite fruit, chocolate, whipped cream or whatever you like. Or, of course, you can eat it as is.

ACKNOWLEDGEMENTS

First of all, thank you so much to my readers. I have met some wonderful people through my writing. My readers are some of the most caring and thoughtful folks I have ever been in contact with. I thank you for your continued support of my dream.

Thanks once again to Julie Hatton, my cover designer. She brought Landry and Zep to life in such a gorgeous cover.

Thank you to my fellow authors. In case you didn’t know, your support and valuable insight mean the world to me. I am especially thankful to KC Hart, Ami Diane, Shonda Czeschin Fischer and Sharon Brownlie. They are always there when I have crazy questions and they make my inquiries seem perfectly normal.

To my friends. There just aren’t words to describe how much I am thankful for you all. Some of my most supportive readers are ones that I graduated from high school with. (We won’t say how long ago.)

To my husband and daughter. Thank you both for going on this ride with me. Your support means the world to me and I’m sorry about all the craziness you have to put up with. Thank you for just shaking your heads and walking away when I start talking to myself. I love you MORE!

ABOUT THE AUTHOR

Jamie Rutland Gillespie was born and raised in a tiny, country town in South Carolina. At the age of 18, she moved to a slightly larger town in the same state and still lives there. She spent much of her youth visiting the beaches of the low country and taking trips to the mountains of North Carolina and Tennessee. The mountains were always her "happy place" and she still visits there whenever she has the chance.

Jamie has always loved to read. She got her library card at the small library in her hometown at the age of 6. She has a vivid imagination and has always made up stories of places, people and situations that exist only in her head.

She currently lives in South Carolina with her husband, daughter and her 17 year old YorkiePom, who is her baby. She is still an avid reader and loves writing books, doing crossword puzzles, baking and spending time with her family.

A Sneak Peek at the first chapter of the next book in the series:

Witching For Murder

Chapter 1

October in the mountains is wonderful. The leaves are at their peak color and the temperatures are perfect; chilly at night and warmer during the day. This was the time of year that enticed so many tourists to visit. All the shops on Main Street had started decorating for Halloween and people just seemed to be happy all of the time.

Landry Burke owned the Magnolia Place Apartment building, as well as the bookstore across the street from it, Jasmine Bloom Books. She and her staff at the bookstore had ordered brand new decorations and were going to start putting them up today.

Landry woke up and turned off her alarm. She intended to lay in bed a few minutes and cuddle with her puppy, Zep, who was named for one of her favorite bands. That was until she heard her name being yelled from the other part of the apartment. It was then she remembered her mother, Claire, was visiting. She got up and went to the kitchen.

"How does this thing work? I am in desperate need of coffee and I can't figure out what to do." Claire threw her hands up in the air and plopped down in a kitchen chair.

Landry walked over and made the coffee and turned it on. Claire was used to having people do it for her since she spent most of her time these days traveling to other countries and living a life of leisure. She had inherited a boatload of money from an aunt and was using it to fund her extravagant lifestyle. Landry had also inherited money from her own late aunt but she was still living the sort of life affording a librarian, since that was her job before she moved to Bobwhite Mountain, TN to take over her Aunt Tildie's estate.

"Mother, you should probably watch what I'm doing in case you ever need to make the coffee yourself, you know." Landry knew it was a lost cause but she tried anyway.

"I'll worry about that if and when it happens. What are you doing today? Maybe we can go sightseeing or something." Claire smoothed her morning hair down.

"Sorry, but I have to work. Ms. Millie is coming in late today since she has an early doctor's appointment so I have to open the bookstore. Besides, we're going to start decorating for Halloween today. I've been looking forward to it. You're more than welcome to come help if you like." She had to turn her face away when she said it so Claire couldn't see the wry smile on her face.

"I hardly think so. Why don't you hire someone to do that for you? Surely you've more important things to take care of." Claire laughed.

"Nope, I want to do it. It's fun to decorate myself. When our customers come in and rave about how good it looks, it makes me proud of what we did." Landry handed Claire her coffee just as Zep walked into the kitchen.

"I'm going to take Zep for a little walk before I eat breakfast. I thought I would make us some bacon and eggs this morning. Sound good to you?" she asked Claire as she put Zep's leash on him.

Claire sighed. "I suppose so. Why don't we just order something in? No sense in you making a mess in the kitchen."

"I like to cook, mother, especially when there's someone else here to eat with me. We'll be right back."

As she took Zep on his walk, she thought about how different she and her mother were. Claire would be perfectly fine not having to lift a finger to do anything. She loved having others do all the work. Landry was more like her late aunt, Claire's sister. Aunt Tildie worked hard at everything she did. She'd been a librarian for the first part of her life and was, in fact, the reason Landry became a librarian. Then Aunt Tildie had bought and run a working farm, for goodness sakes. She harvested crops, canned them, and even helped to take care of the cows and other animals on the farm. How could two sisters be so different, she wondered. She also wondered just how long Claire planned to stay with her.

She got back to the apartment and made breakfast. They ate and Claire told her she was going to browse through downtown for a while. "By the way, who did you say bought Tildie's farm?" she asked.

"Steve and Denise Wilcox. They're Adam's aunt and uncle. Their daughter, Lisa, is the manager here at Magnolia Place. They're a wonderful couple. Why do you ask?" she turned to Claire.

"No reason, really. I know how much Tildie loved the farm. I was so surprised when she sold it and bought this building and the bookstore. She said it was because she was lonely out there at the farm and she couldn't take care of it anymore. I never thought it was a good idea for a single woman to take on a farm, anyway, but I know she was happy there." Claire got up to go get dressed.

Landry gave Zep some treats for the day and got ready for work. She told Claire goodbye and went down to the lobby, where Garrett and Lisa were already hard at work.

"Hey, Landry," Lisa said. "How's it going with your mother visiting?"

"Actually, not bad. She still has her uppity ways but she seems to be more relaxed than I've seen her in a while." Landry told her. "I'm still not quite sure what brought her here to visit all of a sudden. The last time I spoke with her before she came, she had taken a spill and hurt her back. She told me the medicine she was taking made her unusually sleepy."

Landry told Lisa she had to run. She walked over to the bookstore and opened up. Jenna came in just a few minutes later.

"Good morning, Jenna. I've started the coffee and I thought we could start decorating for Halloween. There are some boxes in the office of new things I ordered and we still have the things from last year. We can go through them and what we don't want to use anymore, we can donate."

"Sounds great. I love decorating and I have a new Halloween candle that smells like pumpkin. I think I'll light it to set the tone," Jenna said.

After Landry had her coffee and Jenna got things ready at the counter in case any customers came in, they started with the decorations. They both laughed with delight at every box they opened. There were so many cute items to decorate with. They had a couple of customers but the morning was relatively slow. Landry was commenting on the orange pumpkin lights when the bell on the front door rang, signifying a customer. She looked up in surprise when she saw it was her mother and Karen Scott. Karen was an author and she rented the one bedroom apartment next to Landry's on the 4th floor of Magnolia Place.

"Hi, mother. Hello, Karen. So nice to see you in town. I didn't realize you were visiting this week." She put the lights down and walked over to greet them.

"Hi, dear. Karen and I are just out browsing Main Street and thought we would stop in to say hello and see how much decorating you have done." Claire spoke up. "Karen and I have become fast friends. Why in the world didn't you tell me about the wonderful people you have living in your apartment building?"

"I'm sorry, mother. Karen is a part time resident of the building. I hope you aren't bothering her since she comes here to get away from people so she can write her next book in peace and quiet." Landry smiled at Karen.

"That's true," Karen replied. "But this time, I'm not here to write. See, I have a book signing over in Asheville this coming weekend. I have some things here at my apartment I need for the signing and, since my husband is traveling for his job right now, I thought I would come and enjoy the town for once. Your mother and I met in the lobby a few hours ago and we hit it off right away. She's a charming woman."

Landry stood completely still for a second. She'd never heard anyone call Claire charming and was at a loss for words. When she finally got her mouth to work, she replied. "Thank you, Karen. I'm glad the two of you are getting along so well."

"Oh, yes, we are. It's like we've known each other for years. In fact, I haven't met anyone that I clicked with so fast before." Claire smiled at Karen and then turned back to Landry.

"It's looking festive here already. This is such a quaint little store. What is that I smell? Do you have something baking in here?" Claire scrunched her nose up.

Jenna said, "Nope. It's the pumpkin scented candle you smell. Ambiance, ya know."

"Yes." Claire almost made the disgusted face she was famous for but must have thought twice about it in front of her new friend. "We must be going now. We're going to try the little diner down the street for lunch. Karen said she orders in from there when she's in town writing and thinks the food is divine." She and Karen turned to leave when Claire turned back around and looked at Landry.

"I almost forgot. I've asked a few people to be at your apartment at 6 o'clock tonight. Make sure you're there, too, please. I have something to tell everyone and I want to give you all time to plan." She looked at Karen and they giggled like little schoolgirls and walked out.

"What on earth is she up to?" Landry thought out loud. "My mother never giggles and she is being so secretive. I have a feeling Karen is involved in it and they just met a few hours ago." She tapped her index finger to her mouth, trying to figure out what it could be.

"No telling," Jenna said. "Wonder who else she's invited to be there tonight?"

Landry shrugged her shoulders and they started with the decorations again. After about an hour, Adam walked into the bookstore. He greeted Landry with a hug and told Jenna hello. He and Landry had started dating each other last month and he was the happiest man alive when he was around her.

"What brings you here?" Landry asked him as she handed him the end of a Halloween banner. "Walk out front with me to put this up."

He carried one end of the banner and got up on the ladder Landry had put outside in front of the window of the bookstore. She had the other end and when he got his end fastened, he got down and moved the ladder to do her end. "Your mother came to my office earlier. I had no idea she even knew where I worked. Of course, she could have asked anyone in town and they would've told her. Anyway, she beckoned me to your apartment at 6pm sharp tonight. Any idea what it's about?"

"Not a clue," Landry informed him. "She came by here to order me to be in my own apartment at the same time. She was with Karen Scott, the author who resides at Magnolia Place part time. They were acting like old chums that had a secret. I guess we'll find out what it's all about tonight." Landry stepped back as Adam started coming down off the ladder. She backed into the board sign they kept in front of the bookstore and went head over heels backwards over it and fell into the holly bushes planted in front of the store.

She screamed when she felt all the sticky leaves prick her skin. Adam ran over and helped her up and saw little dots of blood where the stickers had barely punctured the skin.

He shook his head, smiled and said, "Let's get you inside and clean these off, my little accident waiting to happen."

Landry just rolled her eyes and went inside.

They got her washed up and Adam asked her what time she could get away from the store to have lunch. She told him in about an hour. She wanted to finish the decorations and get the boxes back in storage before Ms. Millie got there after her doctor appointment.

Adam walked over to Magnolia Place and grabbed Zep to take him on a walk while he was waiting on Landry. They walked to the park and Zep laid down on the grass and wallowed in it. He loved the park and, as long as no cats were around, he was such a good doggie. For some reason, he was either infatuated with cats or hated them. He would chase them to the ends of the earth. Luckily, there were no cats here today. Zep got up and shook his whole body from head to toe. He stood there and stared for a minute at nothing and then he started whining for Adam to pick him up. They went back to the apartment building where Adam left Zep on the couch in the den. Landry had left the TV on for him. Zep loved to have the game show channel on while he napped. She had tried to change it up and put the animal channel on one day and he looked at her and whined until she put it back on game shows.

Adam locked up the apartment and went to get Landry. Ms. Millie was there and clicked her tongue when he walked in.

"You should be working instead of taking your girlfriend out to eat, boy."

"Ms. Millie, I work all day. I have to eat; she has to eat. Why shouldn't we eat together?" Adam knew he was getting her goat.

"Just go on. Get outta here before I pinch your ear for talking back to me."

Adam laughed. Ms. Millie had worked in the school cafeteria for 40 years until she retired and she still treated all of the former students like they were in third grade. They all loved it, though. Everybody loved and respected Ms. Millie. She had looked out for all of them when they were young.

He and Landry left and went to the diner to eat lunch. After they sat down in a booth, Landry noticed her mother and Karen were at a table towards the back. They had their heads together and were plotting something. Yep, the secret had to have been put in motion after they friended each other.

"What are you thinking about?" Adam asked when he noticed her not listening to the waitress asking for her drink order.

Landry shook her head slightly and said, "Oh–I'll have a diet cola. Thanks, Velma," she said to the lady who worked there. "Sorry, my mind was elsewhere."

"No problem, hun." She turned to Adam and he told her he would like a glass of lemonade.

"Where was your mind just now?" He looked at Landry.

"Right back there at the table in the back." She pointed and he turned to see her mother and Karen.

"The suspense is killing me," he laughed. "I can't wait to hear what it's about."

"I can. My mother has been known to come up with some pretty off the cuff ideas. I honestly can't believe she and Karen have gotten so close just over the course of a day. But, I don't know Karen at all except for saying hi in passing her in the lobby. She usually goes straight to her apartment and never exits until she's on the way home."

Velma brought out their drinks and got their orders. Before their food came out, Claire and Karen were leaving. They stopped by and told Adam and Landry goodbye and Claire reminded them both to be on time for the meeting she had commanded them to attend.

Be sure to join my author page on FB to keep up with the details of all of my books, including when "Witching for Murder" will be released.

https://www.facebook.com/jrutlandgillespie60

Made in the USA
Columbia, SC
20 October 2023

24198584R00136